About the Book

Here is a spine-tingling collection of devils from round the world which will make you shiver and shake and laugh, too, for it's not always the devil who wins out!

Dorothy Gladys Spicer travels extensively every summer collecting folklore from many different countries. She has gathered this exciting material about all kinds and shapes of devils from Ireland, Germany, Czechoslovakia, the Netherlands, Italy, England, Russia and other far away places. Mrs. Spicer has read from accounts recorded long ago and she has talked to the people to whom these tales have been handed down in the regions where they originated. For many of them, she actually visited the spot where the encounter with the devil is supposed to have taken place.

A marvelous collection of stories to remember and repeat on a dark and gloomy night!

13 DEVILS

by

DOROTHY GLADYS SPICER

illustrated by Sofia

COWARD-McCANN, Inc.   NEW YORK

TO
MARGARET CALLOW

of "Wild Oaks"
whose home is my home in England

Library of Congress Catalog Card Number: 67-10425
Printed in the United States of America

CONTENTS

ABOUT DEVILS

Everyone has his own notion about Devils. Once, when I was a child, a dear old friend told me of the *personal* Devil who plagues everyone. Then I was puzzled, but now I know what he meant. He was referring to the contrary spirit within that makes us do this, or say that—though we know very well it's horrid and mean.

In the popular belief of every country, Devils and demons and wicked imps stand for the evil within man's heart. These creatures are servants of the Master Devil, the Prince of Hell, who sends them swarming over earth. They tempt the man who, from greed for gold, lust for power, or some desperate need, makes a pact and promises his soul—*for a price*.

As I traveled about in search of these tales for *13 Devils*, I learned that Devils come in all sizes and shapes. Some are dapper and young, others gristled and gray. Some get about on foot, while others fly on leathery wings. Then there are Devils like ogres, who have a taste for human flesh. They are the most fearsome of all!

Devils, though wily, aren't always wise. A man may outsmart them, if he uses his head. Then he has his cake and eats it, too. But he must solve a riddle, or turn a trick and either propose, or perform, an improbable task.

The man who fares best, however, is the one who's generous, and does something kind for a Devil. More often than not, he'll return kindness with kindness—for gain or at the expense of another victim. If a Devil can reap a harvest of *several* souls, he'll let one escape. Or he may switch the fate of the generous man, to a person whose soul is wicked and black.

In this collection I've told, in my own fashion, tales of the 13 Devils I fancy most. May they delight you in the reading, as they have me in the writing.

For the Dutch stories of "Hantsje and the Remarkable Beast" and "The Three Clever Brothers," I owe thanks to the distinguished folklorist, A. A. Jaarsma, who heard them from the lips of country folk, in his native Friesland. As with the other tales, I have written these stories as *I* think they happened—in that long-ago time when Devils and demons roamed this earth.

—Dorothy Gladys Spicer

1 THE DEVIL'S APPRENTICE
(Serbia)

Young Vardo's father owned a farm in Serbia's rugged highlands. The soil was too poor to grow full-sized potatoes, too stony to yield full-sized apples and pears. Yet Old Vardo loved the scanty patch he had inherited from his father's father. So long as he could hold on to it, he didn't mind hardships. His son, on the other hand, was restless. No matter how hard they tried, as farmers they'd never get ahead, Vardo grumbled. Now if he could find a master and learn some trade, things might be different. This the lad dinned over and over into the father's ears.

But Old Vardo didn't want his son to leave home. "On the land a man's his own master," the father always said. "Life is hard. We're poor but owned by no man. That's more than most folks with trades can say."

Much as Vardo loved his father, he longed to go into the world and try his luck. At the tavern he had heard all sorts of exciting tales. Old men in their cups babbled of the glittering city of the most glorious Tsar somewhere beyond the first ridge of hills. The city teemed with master craftsmen, eager to teach bright young fellows how to be tailors or blacksmiths or even to make pastries and tidbits for rich men's tables—the old ones said. Life in the city was so grand, they added, that many a youth went there and never came back.

It made Vardo's head spin dizzily. His idea was to come back with a trade. What couldn't he do then! He'd give his father silver coins for his pocket, silver buttons for his vest. And come winter, he'd have a grand new coat, embroidered on the outside and lined with sheepskin.

Mostly Vardo kept his dreams to himself. But one day, when they found blight on the potatoes and worms in the pears, his tongue ran away. "If I had a trade, dear Father," he burst out, "you'd not be worrying about worms! You'd not have to plow and plant this miserable ground, or wonder about our next skimpy meal. Please, Father, let me go to the Tsar's city."

Old Vardo listened with a bowed head. Suddenly he looked up into his son's flushed face and said, "When do you want to go, Son?" He was Vardo's age when he'd asked to seek his fortune. *He* had

7

moped with self-pity and felt trapped for years when his own father refused to let him leave home.

"You'll let me go?" Young Vardo could not believe his ears.

His father clapped him on the shoulder. "Youth must be free," the old man said, and smiled in spite of the ache in his heart. "While you're gone I'll take care of the farm. But when you come back—with that trade of yours, mind you—you'll have to take care of me."

Vardo whooped and embraced his father joyously. "Thank you, thank you, dear Father. You'll not regret letting me go. You'll spend your last days in comfort, you'll see." Then the youth set about to prepare for the journey over the high hills. It turned out not so easy or so short as it had seemed from the farm fields.

Three days later, Vardo plodded wearily to the crest of the topmost ridge. But when he peered all around and didn't see the glittering city of the Tsar, or smoke from any settlement or hut, he felt discouraged and lost. For what with being far from home and nothing but bare heath and thick trees ahead, he couldn't help wondering what might become of him. All those things he had heard at the tavern about masters and apprentices, and how to get rich, might well have been idle tales.

Although Vardo couldn't help feeling frightened, he tightened his belt and headed toward a clump of pines on the slope. But when he got there, everything looked alike. And since, after going this way and that, he was as lost behind as before, Vardo decided to plunge ahead.

After what seemed like a hundred years, he saw a light through the trees and hurried toward it. But once out of the trees, the youth was more frightened than ever. Instead of a hamlet, there was a beach. As far beyond that as eye could see, were waves that rose and fell and thundered against black slippery rocks.

Vardo, who had never seen so much water before, gazed about in dismay. He was wondering what he should do next, when a rasping voice spoke at his side. "Well, who are you? What brings you here?" He was not alone, even if he was in the middle of nowhere.

But when he turned toward the speaker, he was not reassured. For the odd-looking fellow beside him wasn't only dressed all in green; from the close-fitting cap on his head to the shoes on his feet he was green! His skin was green and so were his eyes and also the nails on his skinny claw hands. "You'd better speak up, young man, if you've a tongue in your head, that is," he snapped testily when Vardo continued to gape.

"I—I'm Vardo," the youth stammered, swallowing hard. "I'm

from a farm over the ridge. I'm seeking a Master to teach me a t-trade," he concluded, his teeth chattering in spite of himself. For the green eyes now glowed like embers.

"You're seeking a Master, eh?" the Man in Green said. "Well, then, you don't have to look farther. I'll teach you the trade no one knows if you serve as my apprentice three years."

"Oh, yes indeed!" cried Vardo, but then added uneasily, "But tell me, Master, what is the trade no one knows?"

"Don't ask foolish questions. You'll find out soon enough," the Green Man grunted. "Just do what you're told. You'll not get hurt if you follow directions. Follow me," he bawled, as he leaped to the top of a black jagged rock.

When Vardo clambered up the rock, the Green Man raised his arms. "Jump in after me," he ordered curtly. "When I start swimming, you're to follow."

Vardo blanched. His knees knocked together in fright. "I —can't—swim," he said wretchedly.

"Then learn," yelled his Master and dove into the water.

Thinking his hour had come, Vardo shut his eyes tightly and plunged in. When he found out that instead of sinking, he was floating, he opened them. The Man in Green had nearly reached the middle of the sea. And as the youth soon discovered to his amazement, he could follow him, stroke by stroke.

But just as Vardo was getting used to swimming, the Man in Green stopped. He shot out a long green arm, then snatched at the youth's shirt front with a green claw hand.

Vardo felt himself being pulled down, down, through swirling black waves. How long it took to make the awful descent, he never knew. But after a while he felt something solid under his feet, then a tremendous thump on his back. "Breathe, you fool! Open your eyes!" He heard his Master's voice from far away.

Vardo sputtered and wheezed. When he found he was still alive and could breathe, he opened his eyes. The Man in Green was grinning. His eyes glowed brighter than ever. "Well, now we're here, we'll go inside," he said and pounded on the black ugly door Vardo noticed for the first time.

The portal, made of pink coral encrusted with pearls, was set into a rock decorated with shells the color of a sunset. But there wasn't time to admire the door.

When a toothless hag opened it and bowed low before the Man in Green, he pushed Vardo inside and the door slammed shut.

"I've brought a witless youth from the world above. He wants to learn the trade no one knows," the Man in Green said mockingly. "Teach him well, old woman. In three weeks and a day I'll be back to see what he's learned. And as for you, you lily-livered fish," he added, turning to Vardo and waggling a long green finger under his nose. "You'd better remember what you're told, unless—"

But the Man in Green didn't finish his threat. He vanished suddenly, in a flurry of sparks. "W-who is the Master?" whispered Vardo, trying to keep his voice steady. "What is this place?"

The hag stared at the youth. "Then you don't know? Our Master is the Devil," she croaked. "You're his prisoner, at the bottom of the sea, in the realm of demons and creatures of darkness. You and I are his slaves."

"His slaves," Vardo shouted, staggering back in horror. "Then the trade no one knows is—"

"The Devil's trade," the old one said.

"And I'll never see dear Father again, or the blue sky, or the farm." Vardo moaned, his shoulders shaking.

Something about the youth's hopeless grief moved the old crone to compassion. She had been young and beautiful too, when the Devil had dragged her here to teach her the black arts of a witch. She had learned everything and, with no one to help her escape, was still here. But this boy— A daring plan slowly formed in her mind. "There may be a way for you to get back to earth in time," she said kindly, "I'll help you, if you'll work hard and do exactly as I tell you."

"I'll do anything," Vardo promised, thinking of his father. And then, staring into the old woman's wrinkled face, hopelessness surged over him. "But with the Devil as Master, what can we do?" he asked dully.

"We can outwit him," the crone replied curtly. When Vardo pressed her to learn more, she lighted a candle and showed him to bed.

In the days that followed one another drearily, the old witch took great pains at teaching Vardo. "You must learn *everything*, remember each trick, each magic word. In this lies your only hope of escape," she warned. "And when the Devil comes, as he will often, to check on your progress, you must act dull and confused. Always say you've learned nothing, there's nothing you can remember."

When Vardo asked eagerly, "What then?" and fumbled what he was doing, the old woman rapped his knuckles sharply.

"Mind your work," she rasped crossly. "That is, if you hope to ever get home."

Each day brought the Devil's first visit closer. Meanwhile, the witch taught Vardo such magic as he had not thought lay within even Satan's power. The youth learned to twist sand into ropes stronger than hemp, to make pebbles into pearls, millet seeds into fish. Most wonderful of all, she showed him how a man could transform himself into beast or frog—then back into a man again!

When three weeks had passed, the old woman said, "Tomorrow the Devil will come. Whatever he may say, act like a fool. *Remember, you've learned nothing.*"

The next day when Vardo heard a bang at the door, he sprang to the hearth. The old hag shuffled to let in the Master. Vardo peered stupidly at the contents of the pot on the crane. With a long spoon he stirred the brew round and round. And just before the Devil entered the room, he started to chant,

> "Heigh-ho,
> A dead man's toe,
> Three whiskers from a black rat,
> One shark's tooth,
> Seven fishes' tails,
> Five warts from a dead toad.
> Hippity-hop—may a *live* toad
> Jump from the pot."

"Well, young fellow, what are you doing?" bawled the Devil from the door. "In three weeks and a day, haven't you learned that simple trick?"

Vardo let his spoon clatter to the hearth. But when his eyes met the blazing eyes of the Man in Green, he didn't have to pretend fear. "Alas, no, Master," he whined. "I can't do it though I've tried and tried, stirred and stirred. Three days ago I began the brew. The live toad hasn't come out yet." Collapsing in a heap on a stool, he sobbed noisily.

"Get up, fool," bellowed the Devil, and poked at Vardo with a green foot. "Stop your blubbering. Tell me what you have learned."

"N-nothing, Master. Nothing at all," Vardo moaned. "But I try."

"And you'd better continue, bonehead," roared the Devil. "If you don't learn anything, and I send you back to earth—" He broke off, shaking his fist. Then he turned on his heel and stormed from the room shouting, "I'll be back soon."

At the door, Vardo heard the Master yell, "If you know what's good for you, old woman, you'll teach the nitwit something!"

Vardo laughed aloud. And when the crone returned, rubbing her hands in glee and saying, "I couldn't have done better myself, lad," he applied himself with new zest to learning the Devil's trade.

In the weeks and months that followed, each time the Man in Green came and demanded to know what he'd learned, Vardo acted even more clumsy and bewildered. "Alas, nothing, Master," he'd mumble foolishly. "I . . . just . . . can't . . . remember . . . a . . . thing."

The duller the youth behaved, the greater was the Master's fury, and the more the witch encouraged Vardo. Then one day, after three years of intensive training, the crone warned him, "By now he's convinced you're the stupidest youth in the world. Soon the Devil will cast you into the dark waters outside. Remember how to breathe and swim and you'll reach the world above. But once there, take care. The Master will destroy you, unless you outwit him by the tricks of his own trade."

Vardo's heart beat wildly. "If I do get back to earth again, it will be all because of you," he said gratefully. "I shall remember everything—only I wish I could help you," he added.

"For me it is too late," the crone said, turning away quickly. "You are young."

At last the day came when, as the old one predicted, the Master's frayed temper gave way completely. "Idiot—fool!" he bellowed. "When you were on earth, were you ever able to learn anything?"

Vardo stared vacantly. "Not that I can remember, Master," he replied with a silly laugh. "At least, if I did, I soon forgot it."

"Well, you'll not forget this," shouted the Devil. And before Vardo could step aside, he grabbed the back of his shirt, shook him like a rag and booted him to the door. Then he threw him into the swirling waters without. "Get out of my sight, you feebleminded simpleton—puddinghead—dolt," the Man in Green screamed, in a voice so terrible that fish scurried to shelter under rocks and coral reefs.

As black waves swirled over his head, Vardo heard the Devil thunder, "See if you remember how to reach the world above. And if you do, you'd better not let your path cross mine!"

How Vardo managed to reach the surface he wasn't sure, except that he followed the old witch's instructions. But later, when he awoke on the beach and saw a patch of blue overhead, and foam breaking into a hundred thousand diamonds on the waves, he shouted, "I'm alive! I'm going home. I'll see dear Father again."

By following the sun, Vardo was able to reach the ridge. As he looked down the other side and saw green rolling hills, smoke rising from chimneys, and grazing sheep, the horror of his years with the Devil vanished. And when he saw his father running toward him and heard him sob, "My son, my son, is it really you? When you didn't return, I believed you dead," Vardo knew he was the happiest youth in the world.

"It's really I, dear Father," Vardo cried, hugging his father. "I'm home to stay. And what's more, I've learned a trade—the trade no one knows." After Young Vardo had related his adventures, he ended, "I'll show you soon, dear Father, how well I've learned my trade. You'll not have to worry about making ends meet!"

But Old Vardo couldn't help being uneasy. No good ever came from dealings with the Devil. Yet, with the boy home alive and well, not even the Devil or the trade he had taught his son mattered.

A few days passed and then Young Vardo burst into the kitchen. "Father, Father," he shouted. "You and I are going to the fair at the village of Goyko. We'll trade with the best, see pretty girls and stuff ourselves with sausages and sweets."

But Old Vardo didn't even glance up from the watery soup he was stirring. "We're poor, Son," he said severely. "We've nothing to trade, not even a hen. As for sausages and sweets, you seem to forget, between us we haven't the price of a mug of ale."

"But you seem to forget I've learned a trade." Vardo chuckled and pulled his father to the door. "On the way to Goyko, I'll explain my plan. I'll show you what I can do."

On the dusty road to the fair, Old Vardo was still sputtering about the irresponsibility of youth when his son interrupted, "Listen carefully, dear Father," he said. "My new trade enables me to do remarkable things. Now I shall change myself into a horse for you to lead by a halter around my neck."

"You *what!*" shouted the old man.

Young Vardo grinned. "In a minute I'll be the most spirited high-stepping stallion you or anyone has laid eyes on," he said, enjoying himself hugely. "Everyone at Goyko will want to buy me. But don't sell—not until a red-faced Turk blusters up with his bag of gold."

"A bag of gold—for a horse," gasped Old Vardo.

"Yes, but don't take one bag of gold when he offers it," the youth replied. "The Turk—my old Master, the Devil, in disguise—will haggle and bargain. When he offers three bags, give him the horse, but keep the halter, unless you want me to remain a horse forever," he added with a wink and concluded, "Strike the ground with the halter three times, and you'll find yourself home. And I'll be there to welcome you."

So saying, Vardo vanished and in his place a handsome black stallion pawed at the ground. The old man reached for the halter. Later, when he led the beast with fiery eyes and flowing mane into the marketplace at Goyko, everyone gaped and crowded around. People admired the creature at a distance and some made bids. But the shabby peasant refused all offers. "There's not another horse in the world like mine," he said. "I won't sell until I get my price."

"Your price, eh?" boomed a voice from the fringes of the crowd. "Well, in that case, perhaps this gold will change your mind, old man." With that, a Turk in baggy red trousers and richly worked vest elbowed his way forward and tossed a bag of gold before Old Vardo.

The old man did not even glance at the money. "One bag of gold won't change my mind. This horse is worth more, much more." The throng "Oh-ed" and "Ah-ed" in astonishment. And when the fellow refused two, they gasped in dismay.

"Swindler! Cheat!" roared the Turk, purple with rage. Then he slapped down yet another bag.

"The horse is sold," Old Vardo announced and picked up the gold. The Turk grunted. He reached for the halter, but before he could grasp it, the old man stepped aside. "I said the horse," he shouted, and struck the ground three times with the halter.

As by magic, the Turk disappeared, and so did the horse. In the wink of an eyelash Old Vardo was back in the kitchen. The gold was there, too, and Young Vardo was thumping his back. "Well done, dear Father," the youth whooped. "Well done."

The next time Vardo suggested a visit to the fair at Goyko, his father was at the door before the words left his son's lips. "What are you changing yourself into today?" the old man asked eagerly.

"A gold casket, fitted with a gold key," chuckled Young Vardo and went on to explain that, as before, many would wish to purchase the object. "But refuse to sell until my Master, the Devil, comes along disguised, this time, as a rich Venetian. Agree to sell the box for seven bags of gold but by no means part with the key," he warned. "Hurl that to the ground and all will be well. But should my Master snatch the key from you—" he added with a worried frown.

"Never fear, Son," interrupted Old Vardo. "I'll take care of the key."

At the fair everything happened exactly as the youth had predicted. Everyone stared at the gleaming casket. Many asked to touch the diamonds and rubies that encrusted the lid, to turn the wonderful key. All longed to own the box, but no one could pay—no one, that is, until along came a Venetian, in purple robes and a ring that flashed like fire. When he muscled his way through the crowd, the throng gaped in awe.

The Venetian offered first three bags of gold, and then four, and five, and finally SEVEN before the old man shouted, "Sold!"

Vardo's father handed over the casket, taking care to remove the key from the lock. But just as he was going to hurl the key to the ground, the Venetian wrenched it from his hand. "Don't imagine you'll fool me a second time, old man," he sneered and held up the prize.

Now when he snatched the key, the casket vanished and so did the Venetian. The next moment, Old Vardo saw a white dove mount higher and higher into the sky. A monstrous hawk with twitching claws followed in screeching pursuit. "My son, my son, what have I done?" moaned the old man, wiping his eyes. When he looked again all he saw were two specks—one white, the other black—with the distance between growing less steadily.

It was soon evident to Vardo that, as the dove, he was losing ground to the hawk—three times bigger, three times as strong. As they sped on over hill and dale, over villages and town, Vardo wondered what magic he could devise to escape his old Master's vengeance.

It wasn't until Vardo peered down desperately and saw the golden turrets and towers of the Tsar's city and the royal gardens directly below that the idea came to him. For in the garden walked a young maiden, the Princess Yelitza. Uttering a shrill cry, the dove dropped down just as the girl looked up. When she held up her hands to shelter the bird, it changed into a bouquet of flowers more beautiful than any she had ever seen.

Meanwhile, the hawk, whose black ugly claws had all but clutched the white tail of the dove, uttered a hoarse scream of rage. Then the hawk vanished. "Now you're safe, little dove," whispered the Princes Yelitza and held the bouquet to her bosom.

But Vardo wasn't safe, as he well knew. The tricks of the Devil aren't easy to thwart. No sooner had the hawk disappeared than Satan stood at the gate, in the guise of a bleary-eyed beggarwoman carrying a basket of simples. When the Princess ran past her, to show her father, the Tsar, her bouquet, the old beggar whined, "Please, please, beautiful Princess. One flower, I beg you, to cure the sick, ease the dying."

"These flowers fell to me from Heaven. You can't have them—you or anyone," cried the Princess.

"Give her a flower at once, Yelitza," ordered the Tsar sternly, for he was standing in the courtyard, unnoticed. "She wants to make medicine."

"I'll not do it!" the Princess said and stamped her foot. "These flowers are mine. I'll not part with even one."

The Tsar blanched in anger and reached for the bouquet. The beggarwoman's eyes flared with strange light. And things might have gone hard with the Princess Yelitza, save for the event that followed.

For the flowers in the bouquet suddenly changed into a hundred thousand grains of wheat. And as for the whining beggar, she became a greedy hen, followed by seven greedy chicks. The hen and her brood gobbled at the grains. "Stop them—stop them!" cried Yelitza, clasping her hands in anguish.

But before anyone could stop the strange goings-on and all but one grain of wheat had disappeared, *it* changed into a fox. The fox leaped at the hen. At one gulp he swallowed the creature. Then he gulped down the chicks, first one—then three—and finally seven.

No sooner had the hen and her brood disappeared than the fox vanished, also. The next instant, a handsome young man was bowing low before the astonished Tsar and the Princess Yelitza.

"Who are you?" thundered the Tsar.

"I am Vardo," the young man replied, and added, flashing a smile at the Princess, "You see, I had to outwit the Devil."

"Outwit the Devil!" the Tsar roared angrily. "Perhaps you'd better explain, young man."

But when Vardo had related his adventures as the Devil's apprentice and all that had taken place since, the Tsar slapped his thigh and laughed until tears of mirth coursed down his cheeks. "So," he chortled, when he could speak, "you've outwitted the Devil with the Devil's own tricks."

"Yes, your Highness, and I don't think the Devil will come back again," Vardo said modestly, his eyes on the face of the Princess.

"Then you were the dove in the sky," Yelitza whispered. "And the bouquet that fell from Heaven to me."

Now when the Tsar saw how things were between his daughter and the young man, he was mightily pleased. "A lad who's clever enough to drive the Evil One away is clever enough to marry my daughter," he said, and blessed the young pair.

Then Young Vardo sent for Old Vardo. And when he saw his son well and alive, and the beautiful girl he was to wed, the father's joy knew no end. He embraced the youth and made him promise he would never practice magic arts again. "No good comes from dealings with the Devil," Old Vardo said.

And Vardo never did, though he couldn't help thinking of the poor old witch and wishing he could bring her up into the world again. "We owe all our happiness to her," he said, after he and Yelitza were man and wife.

"Hush, my darling," comforted Yelitza. "You can do nothing for her now. She told you herself it was too late."

Vardo and Yelitza lived happily to the end of their days. And the old Tsar was proud of his son. "When I'm dead and gone, he's clever enough to rule in my stead," the ruler confided to Old Vardo.

And Old Vardo smiled, proud as a peacock of his beautiful daughter. "With such a wife, he's bound to succeed!" he agreed and winked at the Tsar.

2　OLD NICK'S BRIDGE
(England)

The young cobbler Jack was the cleverest shoemaker in the whole valley of the River Dibble, in Yorkshire's West Riding. His grandfather had taught the youth his trade. When the old man died, he left him both the business and his gray stone cottage.

Jack was a big lusty young man with a boisterous laugh and a fondness for joking. He was high-spirited, too, especially when not quite sober. Yet, in spite of his faults, Jack had a generous heart. He never turned from his door a hungry dog or cat—or a man with holes in his shoes, but naught in his purse. The youth liked his work and took pride in his craft. And whether patching a clodhopper's boot or mending a lady's slipper, he did his task with skill. "When Jack's done, a body must put on spectacles to see where the hole was, the patch starts," clucked the folks roundabout Thorpe Fell Top.

Jack never lacked work. Rich and poor alike came to him. But he always went to the monks at the Abbey, thirteen miles distant, to fetch a sack of worn sandals and then take them back in repair. "The Brothers give me more work than all the villagers together," Jack said. For what with pilgrimages to holy places, and tending vines and plowing at the Abbey, their sandal soles flapped like an old crow's wings.

The young cobbler liked the monks, especially Brother Jucundus. Though Jack wasn't pious himself, and was aware of his own faults, with them he felt comfortable.

The thirteen miles to the Abbey was a right good piece for a man with a sack. Yet the youth didn't mind the distance, or the load, or even fording the Dibble which had no bridge. At the riverbank Jack always rolled up his breeches, took off his boots, and waded across. In spite of the bother, it was a treat to go to the Abbey. Jack's welcome was hearty. Besides, he could count on Cook to provide a tasty bite in the kitchen. Sometimes, when a storm blew up or dusk closed in, the Brothers even insisted he stay the night.

One day when he called at the Abbey, the sandals were so frayed Jack scratched his head. "If only you'd give me your sandals in time," he complained to Brother Jucundus. "I'd add seven years to their life."

"And if only you'd beware of the Devil, my son, and give God your soul in time," said the Abbot sharply, swishing by with his rosary, "Saint Peter would let you through the gate."

Jack stared after the white-robed Abbot's spare form and winked at Brother Jucundus. "What with the Holy Father to pray for me, and also the monks, I've no need to worry, eh?" he asked.

"Hush, Jack. Don't joke," Brother Jucundus sighed. "The Father's upset. He's heard of the brawl last week at the tavern—the blows—the ugly words."

"Ah me," Jack said and hung his head in shame. "He won't be hearing of such goings-on again."

"Well, off with you, then," Brother Jucundus said. A smile creased his ruddy face as he helped Jack tie up the sack. "If you can stretch the life of these sandals by seven years," he chuckled, "I daresay Saint Peter won't quibble when you reach the gate!"

With a loud guffaw Jack slung the sack to his back. "Expect me soon," he bawled over his shoulder as he trudged up the hill. "I'll bring them back better than new."

And Jack did his best, though the sandals were in a woeful state. When he took them back, later, and dumped them into the middle of the courtyard, the monks gathered around with "Ohs" and "Ahs" of delight. "No cobbler in the world can perform such miracles," declared Brother Jucundus. "And since all work and no play makes Jack a dull boy, you must be our guest for today and go home tomorrow."

Jack needed no coaxing. That night he dined with the monks on fresh trout from the stream. And with bread fresh from the oven and wild strawberries from the forest, no feast was finer. Finally, when the Abbot ordered Brother Jucundus to fetch a bottle of the old Malmsey he reserved for special guests, the feast became an occasion.

Shortly after supper, Brother Jucundus lighted a candle. "Come," he said to Jack. "At the Abbey it's early to bed and early to rise," and led him down a long corridor to a cell. "The place is small, for one so big," he said kindly. "The bed's hard. God bless your sleep. Rest well, my son."

And Jack did—so well that he was still snoring when Brother Jucundus shook him awake at dawn. After a hurried breakfast, the monks, who'd changed their worn sandals for the mended ones, had as great a load for Jack to take home as the one he had just brought. He had just tossed it to his broad shoulder and was bidding his hosts farewell when out rushed the cook. In one hand he waved a bottle of wine, in the other, an eel pie.

" 'Tis far you must go—" puffed Cook. "Too far for a man without a bite on the way." Then nothing would do but Jack must open the sack, so he could place the food on top of the worn sandals.

Jack thanked the Brothers and bounded up the hill. As he passed the Abbey mill and the ancient yews, Jack was so happy he started to whistle. Striding across the long stretch of heath, the miles melted like mist on the heather. Before he knew it, he'd passed Pateley Bridge and Burnsall Parish. At last he saw the Dibble, shining like silver in the sun.

Jack broke into a run, and burst into song. By the time he'd reached the grassy bank and kicked off his shoes, his lusty voice drowned out bird songs and the noise of rushing water in the river bed. As Jack plunged into the Dibble and splashed across, he was still singing. When he clambered up the bank toward a fallen log, he was belting out these words at the top of his lungs:

> "As I walked the highway
> Along came Old Nick.
> And thus did he say,
> 'Sing, Link-a-down-dilly,
> Heigh-down, Ho-down derry—' "

At that very moment, a voice close at hand snatched the words from Jack's lips. The refrain thundered up and down the Dibble:

> "Tol-lol, ferol, derol-do,
> Dol-lol, derry-do."

Jack's jaw dropped. He glanced quickly this way and that. Seeing no one, he couldn't help feeling uneasy. He sat down on the log to think matters over and dry his feet in the grass. Jack had barely settled when a chuckle beside him made him jump.

When he saw the swarthy fellow in the black smock at the other end of the log, Jack was terrified. And that was before he noticed the horns, the round bulgy eyes and the forked tail curled over his back.

"Don't be afraid. I didn't mean to scare you," the swarthy fellow said so kindly that Jack felt somewhat reassured. "I hope you didn't mind my chiming in, when I saw we shared a taste in songs."

"N-no," stammered Jack, trying to conceal his shakiness. After all, with the Horned One smiling so pleasantly, his manners so polite, Jack was almost ashamed of his fright. "Who are you?" he asked, though he knew well enough.

"Old Nick himself," laughed the Devil, his eyes beaming like carriage lights. He laughed at the joke so uproariously that Jack couldn't help joining in.

Once they'd laughed together, Jack's terror seemed to vanish. The longer the two sat side by side, the more he discovered he liked his companion. He joked and told stories, and taught Jack merry songs he'd not heard. Time slipped by quickly. Suddenly Jack was hungry. He'd not eaten since morning.

By now, Jack almost felt he'd known Old Nick a lifetime. Still, he didn't want to seem forward. But at last he screwed up his courage to say, "Since we share a taste in songs, I wondered if—if you'd—" He stopped to swallow.

Old Nick's manner changed abruptly. "If I'd what?" he snapped, his eyes glittering. He'd never met a human who, sooner or later, didn't bargain and haggle for something or other.

"If, since you're so kind, you'd care to share my lunch," Jack said, diving into his sack. "If your taste is the same in wine and eel pie, that is," he added, for his companion was staring at him in an odd way.

"Kind, eh?" grunted the Devil, more pleased than he cared admit. No one had ever called him kind. Besides, now he came to think of it, no one had ever been kind to him, or offered anything without expecting a handsome return. A warm glow came into the bulgy eyes. "Well, what are we waiting for, lad?" he shouted. "I'm hungry enough to eat a dozen eel-pies and drain a dozen bottles of wine."

Now whether it was the warmth of the sun, or the warmth of the wine—or his companion's cleverness—that gave Jack the idea, we don't know. But after a while, he got to thinking 'twas a pity, surely, that neither the Abbot nor Brother Jucundus—or his cronies at the tavern—would ever believe how kind, and how much of a gentleman, the Devil really was. They'd not even believe that he, Jack, had met him. They'd say, "The cobbler's been tippling."

Jack's merry face clouded. What he needed was proof—proof of his adventure, something to show what he said was true.

"Well, speak up, lad. What's on your mind?" asked the Devil, his brow darkening. For Jack, who was wool-gathering, didn't laugh at his jokes anymore. He was like the others, Satan decided—scheming, conniving. So, like the others, he'd pay with his soul.

But when Jack tried to speak, the cat got his tongue. He twisted at a button and opened his mouth. The bright flickering eyes didn't make speaking up easier. "I was wondering if—if—since you're so powerful—" Jack said and stopped, abashed by his own boldness.

"WELL?" bawled Old Nick, his tail twitching.

"If you'd do something like building a brigg [bridge] over the River Dibble—something good," blurted Jack. "Then, when the Abbot and the monks tell me you're wicked, I can point to the brigg and say, 'He's good, too—when he chooses.' Then they'll not say I was drunk, when I tell about meeting you."

At first, Old Nick was too stunned to speak. The simple fellow wasn't like the rest. Satan chortled, then rubbed his hands in glee. After all, why not? If he did as Jack proposed—and let Jack off— the harvest of souls would be doubled. If stupid folks believed the Devil was capable of goodness as well as wickedness, and proof was there—ha— "Come back in three days," he said. And when Jack looked again, he had vanished.

When Jack returned to the Dibble three days later, lo! the river was spanned by as fine a saddleback bridge as any in Yorkshire. From far and near people came to gape, to marvel as to how the bridge came there. " 'Tis a miracle," declared the Abbot who brought his monks to inspect the wonder and give thanks to God.

But when Jack told the Holy Father what had really happened, and recounted his adventure with Old Nick, the Abbot shook his head. "Remember what I said, my son," he replied sternly. "Commit your soul to God in time."

As for Jack's cronies at the tavern, they roared with laughter at his story. "It's easy to tell what you were doing, coming home that day," they scoffed.

"Then how do you explain the brigg?" countered Jack.

Only Brother Jucundus believed the youth. When Jack asked, "Do you think the Devil's all bad?" it was as though a candle burned behind the monk's ruddy face.

"No, my son, though I used to," the Brother said. "Now I'm convinced no one's all bad, even the Devil, with his wickedness. But it's taken a good man to teach me the lesson," he added, staring at Jack as though seeing him for the first time.

Many years after Jack and Brother Jucundus and the other monks at the Abbey had gone to their rest, the mysterious bridge was standing over the Dibble. Many said the Romans had built it. But to this day, the folks around Thorpe Fell Top know better. In the course of time they came to believe Jack's tale. "Old Nick himself built the bridge," they say, and point to some remnant of stone.

3

HANTSJE AND THE REMARKABLE BEAST
(Netherlands)

In Friesland, Holland's most northerly province, goblins and ghosts, and Devils especially, once slid through the mists and lurked in the forests. These creatures were wicked and mean, but of them all Hantsje was the wickedest Devil who ever climbed up into the world from the depths of Hell.

Many tales were told of Hantsje, and, as a lad, the young farmer Pieter had heard most of them, tales that gave him night-mares for weeks. "If ever you meet him, keep your wits about you," his grandfather warned him, over and over. "Hantsje is sly, but he's also stupid. When he starts to haggle, you can trick him. And trick him you must if you're to hold on to your soul," the old man concluded, rolling his china-blue eyes heavenward.

What with inheriting the farm when Grandfather died, and taking a wife, Pieter forgot about Hantsje until the day they met face to face.

That day—the next after *Pinkster*, or Whitsun—began as usual, at dawn. Pieter's golden-haired wife, Anna, poured out tea for his hasty breakfast. "Today's for plowing, love," Pieter said, craning at the sky. Smiling, he buttoned his jacket and started toward the field.

The morning was fine, the earth sweet with spring, and Pieter set to work happily. He made the furrows straight and clean until the plowshare stuck. After he'd wrenched it this way and that, with nothing to show for his pains, the young farmer muttered crossly and dropped to his knees in the furrow.

Pieter scrabbled awhile for what he supposed was a stone, and then his fingers closed on something smooth and round. "Ah-ha, now I have you," he whooped, and tugged and hauled at the mulish thing.

Pieter gawked when he discovered he was clutching not a stone, but a heavy earthen crock. His fingers trembled with excite-ment as he rubbed off the dirt on his pantaloons and then pried up the lid. When the glint of gold met his eyes, he let out a hoarse cry of joy. "Treasure—gold—here in my own field! A hoard of coin buried long ago. What luck!"

Pieter threw his jacket on the ground and dumped out the

coins. He counted them over three times, to be sure. "Three hundred and three shining gold pieces—think of that!" he whispered.

Pieter clicked the coins through his fingers and examined each in turn, before putting them back into the jar. His eyes sparkled at thought of what he'd do now. With a new roof on the old barn, a herd of black-and-white cows and that strip of meadow beside the stream old Popke would surely sell, he and Anna would have the finest farm for miles around. And now he could buy Anna anything her heart desired.

Still in a happy daze, Pieter rose. He slipped on his jacket and pressed the crock closer. "I can't wait to show Anna our treasure," he shouted.

"That treasure is mine," a harsh voice from behind grated.

Pieter spun around. When he found himself staring into a pair of wicked eyes that glowed like candles in a dark room, his heart dropped to the bottom of his wooden shoes. He didn't need to be told this was Hantsje! Grandfather had described him a thousand times—those horns, the long tail forked at the end, the flaming eyes.

"Hand over my crock," Hantsje ordered, switching his tail.

Pieter's voice caught in his throat. "Y-your crock!" he stammered, holding on to it tightly. He was so terrified that his knees knocked together. Still, he was determined not to give up the gold without a fight. "I found this treasure in *my* field, on land my grandfather left me," he said. "What's more, my grandfather inherited it from his father's father, whose grandfather, in turn, gave it to him. What's on my ground belongs to me alone," Pieter added, seeming to gain strength from his recital.

"What's on it, yes," Hantsje admitted grudgingly. "But everything under the ground belongs to the Devil. Even a simpleton knows that. Our kingdom lies down, down, inside the earth. Therefore, all that earth holds belongs to us. Only the foolhardy steal what is ours," he added with a leer.

To cover his fear Pieter bellowed, "Foolhardy or not, this is my treasure and I intend to keep it."

"That gold is mine," declared Hantsje. "But since you're too stupid to know it, you'll find out the hard way. I'm in good humor, so I'll give you a chance to earn it." The Devil grinned evilly. "I'll give you three tasks. If you can perform them—which no human can—I'll go away and leave you the treasure. But if you can't—" he added menacingly.

"If I can't?" blustered Pieter, in spite of the chill that crept up his spine.

"I get the gold, and also your soul, naturally," Hantsje replied.

For an instant Pieter was too stunned to speak. Then his heart beat more quickly. Hantsje was haggling! All at once he remembered the words of his grandfather, "When he starts to haggle, you can trick him. And trick him you must."

Just thinking of the old man gave Pieter courage, for Grandfather had also said that Hantsje was stupid. So before he knew it, a wonderful idea popped into the young man's head. When he spoke, it was almost as if he heard someone else say coldly, "Have it your own way. Name the first task. But before we get started, we'd best settle on a place for the gold—until one or the other wins, that is."

"One or the other, indeed!" snorted Hantsje, giving the earth a sharp crack with his tail. "I always win!"

"Time will tell," Pieter said and patted the crock. And when Hantsje saw that neither jeers nor threats scared the young oaf, he asked sourly where he proposed to deposit the gold.

"I know the very place," Pieter said, a glint in his eye the Devil didn't like. "In the barn, in the great old trunk my grandfather left me, along with the farm. The trunk's too heavy for ten men to lift, but we'll nail it to the floor, just in case. We'll lock the two locks and turn the two keys," he went on. "You can wear one around your neck on a chain, I the other. That way, if either of us wants to cheat—"

"Cheat, eh?" roared Hantsje. "Nobody cheats the Devil!"

When Hantsje saw the fellow wouldn't do anything till the treasure was under lock and key, he reluctantly consented to go through with his plan. And when everything was attended to properly—with the keys hanging around their necks on chains—Pieter shouted, "Name the first task."

"Your first—and doubtless your last—is a riddle," sneered the Devil. *"How far is it from Heaven to earth?* And since the distance from earth to Hell is great," he added, his eyes flaring, "you'd better be quick."

For an instant Pieter felt the chill again. Then suddenly his thoughts raced back to his grandfather. What was it the priest said when the old man lay dying? *"One foot's in the grave, the other in Heaven."* That was it.

Hantsje was tapping with his hoof. "Well?" he bawled. "Must I wait all day?"

"Longer than you think to take me to Hell!" chuckled Pieter. "From Heaven to earth is but one step, as you ought to know, for long ago you fell the distance."

"You—you—" Hantsje shrilled, his evil face the color of putty. "Meet me at dawn in the field, for your second task." As he stumbled away, his shoulders drooped and his tail dragged in the dirt.

Pieter laughed softly and then turned for home. He could scarcely wait to tell Anna of his adventures—how he'd found the gold and met Hantsje, and made the terrible pact. But after Anna heard it all, she burst into tears. "Take care, my darling," she said. "Hantsje won't forget his humiliation today, and you still have two tasks to go."

"Never fear, love," Pieter comforted his wife. "With my wits about me, things will come out right." All the same, he was worried. It was almost time to get up before he fell into a fitful sleep.

When he arrived at the field next day, Hantsje was strutting up and down. Once more he was confident. He held his tail at a jaunty angle. "I see you're a good farmer," he said at once, not bothering with greetings. "I want to make money. Your second task is to raise me a crop, on shares. You can choose the crop, but I'll choose my share," he added, a cunning smile crossing his face.

Pieter thought swiftly. "I choose barley," he said. "What do you choose for your part of the crop—what's above ground or what's underneath?"

When Hantsje replied, "What's underneath, as you should remember!" Pieter wanted to shout. He had remembered! Besides, the Devil was no farmer. Onions and potatoes, carrots and turnips were his idea of a crop.

"Come harvest, I'll be back to collect everything that's mine," Hantsje now said, and toyed with the key at the end of the chain, the key to the trunk that held the gold.

In the days that followed, Pieter worked with a will. He plowed the field and planted seed. When the young barley leaped from the ground, he and Anna rejoiced. When fan-shaped heads of grain appeared on the tall lusty stalks and the field was a sea of waving grain, they could scarcely wait for harvest.

At last, the day came that Hantsje and Pieter agreed to gather the crop. The young farmer shouldered his scythe and went to the field. Already the Devil was waiting, his swarthy face like a gathering storm. "Greetings!" called Pieter, starting to swing with his scythe. "I see you're here for your share of the harvest."

"My share!" Hantsje screamed, quivering in fury. "Scoundrel—trickster! So you've done it again! You get the grain, I nothing but roots." He tore a handful of barley from the ground and shook the spindly roots under Pieter's nose.

"What's underground is yours, what's on top mine," retorted the farmer, swinging his scythe close to Hantsje's cloven hooves. "Or had you forgotten?" The Devil leaped back so fast that he almost tripped over his own tail. Pieter couldn't help laughing.

"You'll laugh on the other side of your mouth when you hear your third task," Hantsje shrieked in rage, lashing out at the grain with his forked tail. "Come sunup, you're to produce a beast in this field—a beast the like of which I have never seen and the origin of which I cannot guess. Just how funny do you think that is, you insolent oaf?"

Pieter shrugged. "Come sunup, you'll see such a beast. And I trust I'll see the last of you," he bellowed with a boldness he didn't feel.

Long after the Devil had stumped away, Pieter stood leaning on his scythe. For all his brave words, he was frightened more than he had ever been. To outwit the sly fellow by answering a riddle, or raising a crop, was one thing. To produce a beast so remarkable was another matter.

After Pieter told Anna about his third task, the whole thing seemed more hopeless than ever. "My luck's run out," he concluded despondently. "Come tomorrow, Hantsje will drag me to Hell."

"Nonsense! Not if I can help it," snapped Anna, angry at the Devil for threatening the safety of her beloved husband. "I must think." Fury lent wings to her wits. Suddenly she clapped her hands and a smile quirked the corners of her lips. "Neither Hantsje, nor anyone else, will recognize the horrendous beast you'll lead out tomorrow, for I'll be that beast!" Anna declared, her eyes sparkling.

Pieter's jaw dropped. "W-what do you mean?" he stammered, staring at Anna so blankly that she burst into peals of laughter. But when she'd disclosed her scheme, he also laughed until tears rolled down his cheeks.

"You're the cleverest wife a man ever had," cried Pieter and caught Anna in his arms.

"There's no time to lose," Anna said, pulling away, "not if you're to help transform me before sunup into the hideous monster that will scare Hantsje back to Hell!"

Anna began to bustle around the kitchen. First she tied up her golden hair in a cloth. Then she plumped herself out with pillows to make her body appear larger. Last of all, she rolled up her red flannel petticoat and told Pieter to tie that behind. "Now cut open the feather bed," she directed. "Smear me with honey. Then roll me over and over in the gray goose feathers."

All night the couple worked. And when at last Ann stood before her husband as an enormous feather ball, with a smaller ball for a head, and feathered arms and legs, even he had to admit he couldn't recognize his own dear wife. "But this is only the beginning," she reminded him. "Now I'm a bird. Wait till you see the remarkable beast I'll be!"

So saying, Anna dropped to the ground on all fours and hung down her head. "Now untie the cloth and brush my hair over my face," she ordered, uttering a growl that made Pieter jump. "This will puzzle Hantsje—a four-legged beast with a golden mane."

Hantsje arrived at the field with the first streaks of dawn, and only a moment later heard the angry shouts from behind. He whirled about and when he saw Pieter brandishing a stick and tugging at a strange creature on a rope, his jaw dropped. "Ho, there, are you pulling me, or am I pulling you?" the farmer roared at the dawdling animal.

Hantsje peered through the morning mist and stifled a scream. Never had he seen so fearsome a monster. Its body was feathered, like a bird. Yet it stood on four feathered legs. The front ones were shorter. When the creature moved it lurched and humped in most ugly fashion. But its thick mane—which covered the face and swept the ground—shone like gold as the mist lifted and the rays of the rising sun touched it.

Hantsje's tail twitched nervously. Pieter yanked up the animal and called out, "Greetings! We're here at last, my beast and I, though you can see how it balks." He paused to wipe sweat from his brow before he asked, "Are you ready to put a name to it?" and added generously, "You can have three chances, since this is a remarkable beast."

Before he could reply, the beast gave a threatening growl. Hantsje stared around wildly. His eyes bulged with fright. When he tried to think, his mind went blank. "It's—it's—a—"

"A WHAT?" shouted Pieter, enjoying himself hugely.

"An English g-goat, I'd say," Hantsje ventured, naming the first thing that came to mind.

"A goat, eh? Well, I'd say you're wrong—what with all these feathers," bawled Pieter, doubling with mirth. "Never mind, you still have two turns. And to show there are no hard feelings, I'll let you view my animal on all sides," he added slyly.

Hantsje was too frightened to relish the idea. Yet, with the taunting smirk on the farmer's face, the Devil forced himself to walk around the beast once, and then twice. But when the creature took to tossing its mane this side and that, and making gurgling noises, the demon was so flustered he yelled, "It's a wild horse from Tibet."

Pieter spat in disgust. "A horse, indeed," he mocked. "That's twice you've failed. Still, you have another turn. But you'd best keep your wits about you, unless—"

"It's—it's a donkey!" shrieked Hantsje desperately. But the words had barely left his lips when the beast snorted and lunged. A feathered foreleg, with what looked to him like terrible claws, shot out. It snatched the key from the chain around his neck. The next thing Hantsje knew, a sharp kick on the shin sent him sprawling to the ground.

"And you're a bigger donkey than I thought," Pieter roared, leaping upon him with his stick.

It was only after the young farmer had thrashed Hantsje within an inch of his life that he lifted him, screaming for mercy, by the scruff of his neck. "Off my land! Out of my sight!" he bellowed. Then he booted the Devil across the field. "You'll get worse, if you ever come back."

But Hantsje never did, nor from that day did he ever dare show his face in Friesland again. And as for Pieter and Anna, as long as they lived, they and their children and grandchildren enjoyed the gold that had been buried in their field. Not selfishly, mind you, but with a proper tithe to the church, and with charity to their neighbors, and a gift to the beggar who came to the door.

4

THE BOOTS THAT
NEVER WORE OUT
(Finland)

Once on a time, a Devil told his wife they'd leave Hell for a while and visit *Suomi,* or Finland, a land of birch and pine forests and a thousand sparkling lakes and, as the Devils had to admit, a land of men who gave trouble. It was impossible to get the better of them and lure them to Hell for their own destruction.

"In Suomi, we'll get a farm, and take our own animals with us. I'll bargain with a man, fray his temper. And then," gloated the Evil One, his eyes round and bright, "he'll have to bargain with me! Then he will be mine and I'll drag him down to Hell."

Now while the Devil was scheming in Hell, the young Jussi, on earth, was working hard enough for three. His two elder brothers, wearied of the dull life on their father's poor farm, had gone adventuring, one day. And once away, they never returned. Three years had passed, and still no word was heard from them.

But absence makes the heart fonder, so goes the old saying. And the longer they stayed away, the more lustily did the parents praise their remarkable sons. "Our boys have gone into the world to seek fortune and fame," the aged couple boasted. "They'll come back, never fear. And when they do, they'll dress us like rich folks, and feed us fancy cakes and wine."

When people reminded the doting oldsters that meanwhile their youngest son, Jussi, was doing his brothers' work, as well as his own, his father shrugged. "Jussi, ah yes," he said with scorn. He's content to plow and sow, milk cows and feed pigs. He's not one for adventuring and making a fortune."

"As if I wouldn't like to," sighed Jussi. "But with my brothers gone—and our parents so old—my place is here." Then he went to the barn whistling. For Jussi loved his parents dearly, despite their harsh words.

But one night, he had a change of heart. After he'd gone to bed and the old people fancied him asleep, Jussi heard his father say, "Our youngest son isn't like the others. He'll never amount to a hill of beans. All he'll ever do is potter."

"Alas, yes," the youth's mother agreed. "He's not clever enough to seek his fortune or care for us when we can't work."

"Ah, well, he who eavesdrops hears no good of himself," Jussi said sadly. "I'll go away this very night. But I'll be back, come harvest," he added hastily, convinced that his brothers never would return. When his parents were asleep, he threw on his clothes and crept to the door. It would do them good to fend for themselves for a time, he decided.

Outside, the air was crisp, the stars close. "I could pick you like buttercups," Jussi cried joyfully and reached up his arms. Tingling with excitement, he pelted toward the crossroads. He was free—his own man. At last he, too, was going adventuring. "I'll head south, where I'll find farms to work on for food—till I can make my fortune."

The rest of the night and all next day, Jussi slogged along the road. But he saw no farms. As dusk closed in, he was dismayed. His feet were like stones, his stomach a yawning sack. Just as he thought he'd best curl up beside the road, the lad saw a light. "Ho, a farm's yonder," he cried, and quickened his step.

It was then Jussi heard a voice, from somewhere behind, say, "If it's work you want, I'm looking for a husky lad. And I offer good bed and board."

Jussi turned quickly and saw a dark figure step out from the shadows. "Oh!" he gasped. "But you're—you're—" He stopped in fright and in confusion. For the stranger's eyes glowed in the fast-fading light. He had horns and cloven feet and a long twitching tail.

"I'm a Devil, yes, the stranger admitted, chuckling. "But don't be afraid. I'm master here. My wife and I live in the house beyond the hedge. She's fixing soup and stew now, and from the looks of you, you could do with both. Will you come home to supper with us?" he asked kindly.

At mention of soup and stew, Jussi drooled. At the same time, his skin prickled. Yet he'd wanted adventure, and here it was.
"Thank you," he said. "I do need food, and I'd like to work for you."

"I was sure you would," the Devil said easily. "Work starts at dawn. But tonight we'll celebrate our bargain."

Jussi pricked up his ears, though by now he was so tired he knew he would agree to anything. "A bargain, eh?" he asked.

"Oh, nothing, really," the Devil assured him, waving his tail airily. "Whichever one loses his temper first shall owe the other a patch of hide from his back, a patch big enough to sole a pair of shoes. Besides, I'll expect you to do every task I set you—unless you want to give up your soul," he added.

"Well, all right," Jussi agreed, promising himself he'd not be the one to forfeit his skin—and he'd hold on to his soul, too. He was so hungry now, he'd die if he didn't eat soon.

The Devil was already leading the way to the lighted window. When they'd passed the hedge and turned in at the gate, there was the door. As the Master lifted the latch and pushed it open, Jussi found himself inside a cozy kitchen. And when he sniffed the appetizing aroma from the bubbling pot, he wasn't sorry he'd decided to serve the Devil.

Seeing her husband enter with the lad, the Mistress, who was grizzled and gray, stepped forward to welcome him. She seated Jussi at the white scrubbed table and dished out the soup. When she placed the brimming bowl before him, he thought he'd done well by himself.

After the youth had eaten all he could hold, and his head wobbled drowsily, the Master said briskly, "You'll sleep in the shed, next to the kitchen. But first, we'll seal our bargain with honey mead."

Having drunk the mead, Jussi was sleepier than ever. But when he finally stretched out on his cot and pulled up the covers, he mumbled contentedly, "Devil or not, he's not so bad. But he'll not get my hide—" In less than a minute the youth was sleeping soundly.

He was up before dawn, and after a hearty breakfast the Devil pointed to a pile of empty grain sacks. "Carry them to the barn," he ordered. "Before supper, I'll expect you to have them filled with grain and piled on the floor, ready to cart to the mill."

"Yes, Master," Jussi said. Shouldering the sacks, he went off whistling to his task.

But after he'd worked awhile, Jussi discovered something strange. No sooner were the sacks filled and securely tied than the grain trickled away through a mysterious hole at the bottom. After the same thing happened several times, he was convinced this was the Devil's bewitchment. "If the Master thinks I'll lose my temper over *this*, he has another think coming!" the lad said and sat down on a heavy upturned measure, to decide what to do next.

Suddenly, a horrible yowling from under the sacks made Jussi leap to his feet. "Ha," he exclaimed. "So the Devil's cat is clawing holes in the sacks!" Soon grain and sacks were flying as he tore the pile apart. And sure enough, at the bottom, two baleful eyes peered into his.

Before Jussi could grab at the creature, however, she flew at him, snarling. She sank vicious claws into his arm. Faint with pain, he groped out blindly toward the measure. How he managed to lift it, once his fingers closed on the rim, he never knew. But after he'd smashed the thing down on the demon cat's head, she lay limp as an ugly black rag. "Good riddance to you!" grunted the youth. "I'll wager no grain will spill now!"

And it didn't. At last, Jussi was able to fill the sacks. He stacked them, fat and bulging with grain, on the floor of the barn, and then went to supper.

"I must say, Mistress, I never tasted better soup," Jussi told the Devil's wife when she'd filled his bowl three times.

All the while, the Devil stared suspiciously. "I see you have a good appetite, Jussi," he remarked. "Did you fill all the sacks with grain?"

"Oh, yes, Master, I did," Jussi replied, scraping his bowl.

"Did you—did you see anything?" the Devil asked.

"Only a horrid black cat, Master," said Jussi. "But I smashed her head."

"You WHAT?" bawled the Devil. "You killed my cat?"

"Oh, was the nasty thing yours?" Jussi asked, biting into his goat cheese. "She almost clawed off my arm."

"And too bad she didn't," snarled the Devil, his eyes glittering.

"There, there, Master," Jussi soothed. "You'd not be losing your temper, surely, for a dead cat."

"No, I'd not, if that's what you want!" said the Devil, pressing his lips together. After all, the lad had done his task. The Master took his wife by the arm and stumped off to bed without saying good night.

In the morning, the Devil told Jussi to hitch the oxen and go to the forest for logs. "When it's time to come home, I'll send my dog to show the way. You're to follow the same route he takes," he added with a smug smile.

"You can count on it, Master," Jussi said. Swinging himself to the wagon seat, he creaked through the gate, and down the long road. But all the while, he was wondering what scheme the Devil had up his sleeve. "Ah well, we'll find out soon enough," he told the oxen as they plodded toward the woods.

All day, Jussi loaded logs on the wagon. He'd barely finished when he heard a snarl. Then the Devil's dog bounded toward him, baring his sharp long teeth. "All right, we're ready," Jussi cried and snatched up the reins. "You lead. We'll follow wherever you go."

The dog streaked ahead, taking, at first, the same route Jussi and the oxen had traveled. But when he reached the gate, instead of turning in, the creature paused at a small hole in the hedge. He looked back, lolling his tongue. And then, with a howl so chilling it froze the blood in the lad's veins, the dog leaped through the opening. "Ah-ha—so that's the route we're to follow." Jussi sighed. "Everything is bewitched—yesterday the cat, now the dog."

Knowing the dreadful thing he must do, Jussi drove the oxen on till they reached the hedge. Then he cut them to pieces, which he poked through the hole. He pushed the logs through, one by one, and then the wagon, chopped to bits. Last of all, Jussi stretched himself lean and long as a pole. By turning this way and wriggling that, he finally worked his body through the hole in the hedge.

That night at supper, the Devil eyed Jussi sharply and then asked, "Did you do as I said—follow my dog where he led?"

"Yes, Master, I came the same way," mumbled Jussi, his mouth full of fish.

"You m-mean—" the Devil faltered, more disturbed than he cared to admit.

"That I did as you said," replied the lad, wiping his lips on his hand.

"Any fool would have known it was impossible to get through the hole," the Devil said.

"I only followed your instructions, Master, and a bargain's a bargain," replied Jussi.

The Devil's tail quivered. "What did you do with my oxen, my cart?" he demanded.

"Oh, they're out there, Master, beside the hedge—though, of course, I had to cut them up," Jussi said. "You can see for yourself."

By now the Devil, white with rage, leaped forward. But the lad held up his hand. "Tut, tut, Master, take care," he mocked. "You'd not want to lose your temper, and also your hide, for a team of oxen and a cart!"

"No, blockhead, I'd not," blustered the Devil, sitting down suddenly. "Now get out of my sight," he growled, his eyes smoldering with meanness.

Yawning tremendously, Jussi went to his room, but not to sleep. For when he heard the Devil talking in low tones to his wife, the lad strained his ears to catch every word.

"You must kill the boy at once," the Devil's wife was saying. "All he does is plot our ruin, and eat. Besides, if you don't take care, you'll forget and—"

"Never fear," said the Devil with a laugh that made Jussi's flesh creep. "Call me at midnight. I'll lop off his head with my sword while he sleeps."

Jussi shook his head. "I'm not so sure, Master," he muttered and grinned broadly. For while the pair was scheming to kill him, he'd made plans, too.

By midnight, when the Devil's wife hissed, "Psst! It's time now," Jussi had everything ready. Inside the bed, where his body usually lay, he had placed an ironbound keg, and on the pillow a stone.

"What with only moonlight to see by, and covers tucked in all around, it will seem that I'm lying there," chuckled the youth. Then he settled under the bed and started to snore.

And none too soon, for the next instant the lad heard the light click of the Devil's hooves approaching the door. He pushed it open, inch by inch. And when he'd entered the room, he listened intently, then lifted his arm. Jussi snored louder. In the dim light he saw steel flash.

The sword whistled through the air and then, with a terrific WHAM, the Devil brought it down on the stone. Jussi stopped breathing in mid-snore. "What a hard head," the Master grunted, running a thumb along the edge of the sword. "So hard it's made a nick."

Just to be sure the lad was dead, the Devil struck again—this time with such force that sparks flew from the hidden stone. "I've fixed him now," he said. "But I'll take a whack lower down."

With this blow the sword hit the keg. And when it flew apart, with splintering of wood and bursting of iron, the Devil went back to his wife. "He was tough to kill," he said. "But now he's dead, and we're rid of the sly meddling fellow."

Jussi crawled up from under the bed. "Wait and see, Master," he murmured drowsily. Then he cleared out his bed, and slept soundly the rest of the night.

Jussi rose at dawn, to fetch water and build up the fire. When his Devil and his wife beheld him alive and nimble at the hearth, they thought they were seeing a ghost. But the lad was real enough, and with not a scratch on him! "D-did you sleep well?" the Devil asked, unable to keep his teeth from chattering.

"Never better, Master, until midnight, that is," replied Jussi. "Then something dropped from the ceiling and hit my nose twice. And just as I was dozing off, a muscle cramped in my leg."

Shaking with terror, the Devil sent Jussi to the barn and turned to his wife. "We'll go to market at once," he said. "And I'll give him a task that—"

"That what?" snapped the old creature testily. "You said you'd killed him, and now—"

"Now I know steel can't harm him," the Devil said. "Tonight I'll try fire."

Then the Master told Jussi to hitch up the mare. And with his mind still on the fire he planned to use to destroy Jussi, the Devil said, "While we're at market, you're to make the house flaming red."

What he meant was for Jussi to paint the house red, and, of course, he knew this. But what the lad said was, "Flaming red— while you're gone. But that's impossible, Master." Yet, in spite of his pretended dismay, he was considering a daring plan—a plan that couldn't fail.

"Impossible or not, you'd better do it," growled the Devil.

"I'll do my best, Master," Jussi said, watching the Devil crack his whip and rattle from the gate.

When the pair disappeared around the bend in the road, Jussi slapped his thigh and laughed uproariously. "Flaming red, eh? It's not so impossible, Master, as I made out," he said, and went into another gale of laughter.

When he thought the Devil and his wife had reached market, Jussi lighted a brand and set fire to the house. As the flames licked up, the sky glowed three leagues around. "You'll be rushing back soon, Master," Jussi predicted. "And when you do—" he added, fingering the knife at his belt.

It wasn't long before the pounding of hooves on the road told Jussi he was right. "The Master's coming on the mare's back," he said, cocking an ear. "He's left the cart, and his wife, behind." Just then the Devil dashed around the bend, clutching at the mare's mane, prodding her flanks with the forked end of his tail.

Plunging headlong through the gate, the Devil sprang from the horse's back. "What do you mean—burning my house while I'm at market?" he roared.

"Why, Master, I thought you'd be pleased," Jussi said, with a hurt look. "You said, make the house flaming red, and I did. I thought I got a pretty color."

"You—you knothead," bellowed the Devil. "You knew very

well I meant for you to paint the house—all of it." He reached horrible hands toward Jussi's throat. "Wait till I catch you. I'll drag you to Hell and burn you to a crisp."

"Careful, Master," Jussi warned pleasantly. "I've done my task. You're losing your temper, and all for a burning house."

"Yes, I am, and I'm glad!" shrieked the Devil, casting caution aside. "And if you don't wipe that smirk from your face and get out, I'll—I'll—"

"You'll what, Master?" Jussi taunted, for the Devil, beside himself with rage, now choked helplessly. "I'll get out when you've paid what you owe me."

"Paid what I owe you," sputtered the Devil. "For killing my oxen, chopping up my wagon, burning my house? Pay you, indeed!"

Again the enraged fiend reached toward Jussi. But he caught him deftly by the tail and held him as in a vise. "A bargain's a bargain, Master, in case you've forgotten," the youth said. "You have lost your temper and you've admitted it. Now you must pay."

The demon stamped and bawled until the flaming house crashed to the ground. He whined and begged when he saw Jussi draw out his knife. But the lad paid no heed until he'd taken a generous patch of black swarthy hide from his Master's back. "Now that I have enough skin for a pair of soles—and also the tops— of a pair of boots, you'd best go," Jussi advised, releasing the Devil. "And if I ever see your ugly face around here again—"

With a loud yell, the Devil was off, howling all the way back to Hell—and behind him tagged his evil animals. "I'll have no dealings with Suomi folk ever again. The other devils were right," he admitted to his wife, later, when she joined him in the Underworld. "The men are hard to snare—tricky—and too stupid, even, to lose their tempers."

No sooner had the Devil disappeared than lo! a new farm, better by far, rose out of the smoking rubble. As Jussi gazed at the snug house and the fine barn, with pens for the pigs and coops for the chickens, he rejoiced exceedingly. "As soon as I get my boots made and soled with the Devil's hide, I'll go home and fetch the old ones," he said.

When Jussi jogged home, a few days later, in a shiny cart drawn by a gray mare, his parents ran to greet him. And after he'd related his adventures with the Devil, and they'd admired the boots on his feet, his father said fondly, "We missed you, Son. We knew you'd not fail us, though your brothers did."

"They'll not be back," said Jussi gently, for he knew his brothers better than the old people did. "But now you're coming home with me, to a new and prosperous farm."

Those who tell this tale say that Jussi and his parents lived in contentment many a year. And fame of his remarkable boots spread far and wide. "How did you get them?" people asked in wonder, once they'd stared and touched and sniffed at the sturdy black leather.

"By keeping my temper!" Jussi chortled.

To this day, men of Suomi talk of the boots made from the Devil's hide. "They never wore out," they say. "They're somewhere, tramping the countryside. No one knows who the wearer is, now. But he's lucky. For, like Jussi, with each step he scrunches the Evil One down, down, deeper into Hell."

5

THE SLY GYPSY AND
THE STUPID DEVIL
(Russia)

Once upon a time, so long ago no one remembers when, the Devil King temporarily banished a stupid young Devil from the comforts of Hell. "I'm sending you to live on earth awhile, on a farm in Old Russia," the monarch said. "I want to find out if you're too stupid to learn how to bedevil men. Don't come back here until I give permission," he added, his eyes glowing.

Listening to the royal decree, the young demon's horns drooped, and so did his tail. Yet, when the tunnel to the world above suddenly yawned before him, there was nothing to do but step inside. But when he reached earth and saw his farm, with broad rolling fields, a forest for wood and a huge onion patch, he was more dejected than ever. The farm, to be sure, was the most prosperous for miles around. The only trouble was, the Devil was lazy. He hated work, and his farm needed plenty.

One day not long after, the Devil, who was dragging home a sack of meal from the mill, met a gypsy, face to face. "Ho, ho, I'm in luck! You're the very fellow I want for my slave," shouted the Devil. "You're husky and strong. Take this sack to my barn," he added, with a flip of his tail.

Staring into the black ugly face of the Devil, the gypsy didn't fancy serving him, for he didn't like the bright bulgy eyes, or the set of the horns, and least of all, the slender black legs with cloven hooves for feet. But the Devil was impatient. "Well?" he roared. "Will you obey peaceably or must you learn the hard way? After you've served me seven years, I'll release you with wages—so you'll go into the world with a nest egg."

Another flip of the fellow's tail caused the gypsy to decide he'd try to make the best of a bad bargain. "I'll serve you, Master," he grunted and shouldered the sack.

At the barn door, the Devil turned. "I'm warning you, Gypsy, no tricks," he said, and stalked into the house.

Now the gypsy, who was smart as the Devil was stupid, was an unwilling slave. After many days, and weeks, of hard work, he resolved to make life so intolerable for his Master that he'd wish he'd never been born.

The gypsy's opportunity came next day when the Devil roared, "Hi, lazy one, what are you doing, poking at the fire? I want my tea. Stop your mooning and fetch a bucket of water from the well."

Without deigning to reply, the gypsy shuffled off to the well in a field behind the house. He lowered the bucket on the rope and peered down the dark well shaft. But it wasn't until the pail plopped into the water far below that he had the idea—the idea that would scare his Master at least halfway back to Hell.

Without wasting a second, the gypsy set to work with feverish haste, chuckling all the while. He scooped up handfuls of earth and plastered it all over the stones of the well. And when he finally stood back to admire his handiwork, he laughed aloud. Now the well looked for all the world as if some giant had wrenched it out from deep in the ground!

The Devil, meanwhile, fretted and fumed and switched his tail in annoyance. He'd lighted the charcoal under the samovar. It was ready to fill. That stupid slave hadn't brought his water yet. The Devil tapped his hoof on the floor. But as minutes dragged by, and then an hour, and the gypsy wasn't back, the demon set out on a run to the well. At sight of it, the Devil stopped dead in his tracks and his tail stood straight up in amazement. "Hey you—what are you up to?" he yelled, seeing his servant wipe his earth-covered hands on his smock.

"Oh, nothing to upset you, Master," said the gypsy, grinning. "When you called me lazy, you were right. For after I'd let the bucket down, I didn't feel like hauling it up on the winding pulley. Instead, as you see, I hauled up the well! This way," he ended enthusiastically, "any time you want water, I can fill the pail—and save myself work—by tipping over the well!"

The revelation of his slave's strength so terrified the Devil that his horns trembled with fear. "I-I supposed you may as well leave it that way," he chattered, unable to control his voice. Anyone who could pull a stone well out of the earth as easily as a bunch of weeds was dangerous! "Get on with the onion bed," the Master ordered shakily. "This time, I—I'll manage for myself. I don't need much water for tea."

Only when he saw the gypsy tramp away did the Devil dare fill the pail and give way to his fright. His hands shook as with ague. And on returning to the house, he slopped water as his tail switched about nervously. Only after he'd downed seven glasses of strong tea did his teeth stop chattering.

The following day, when the Devil told the gypsy to fetch firewood from the forest, he took care to keep a civil tongue in his head. And he did not notice the length of strong rope his servant snatched up from the floor and hid under his jacket.

No sooner had the gypsy reached the heart of the forest than he threw down the rope and started to laugh. "The Master's scared out of his wits now," he guffawed. "I can't wait to see his face, after what I'll do next!"

Quickly the gypsy tied the rope from one tree to the next. And when the Devil, waiting for his wood, finally ran out to discover why his servant dawdled, his jaw dropped in astonishment at sight of the trees fastened together. "Well, what are you doing now, block-head?" the Master bellowed. "Why are you tying knots, when I ordered you to fetch wood?"

"Oh, that's exactly what I am doing," grunted the gypsy, glancing up with a smile. "I'm just tying the trees together, so I can drag them all home at once. That way, I'll save myself the trouble of coming back, each time you need wood for a fire."

If the demon was frightened before, he was so terrified now that his knees turned to water. "You needn't bother to haul back the trees," he mumbled after a while. "All I need now are a few faggots and twigs and I'll fetch them myself. You'd better get on to hoeing potatoes."

With his tail flapping first to one side, then the other, the Devil never knew how he finally reached home. And once there, he couldn't even drink tea without upsetting the glass. "Oh me, oh my," he moaned, rocking to and fro in an agony of fear. "A servant with the strength of threescore seven men might try to m-murder me!" And the more he thought of it, the worse matters seemed.

At last, unable to bear his burden alone, the wretched creature decided to risk going back to Hell without permission. "The Devil King will forgive me, once he knows the trouble I'm in," he cried.

So saying, the young Devil tapped his hoof on the ground, and when the tunnel to the Underworld opened, he tumbled inside. The next instant, he was in the chamber of the King, wailing, "Help me! Tell me what to do." Then he collapsed in a writhing mass at the ruler's feet and broke down completely.

"How dare you come here without permission and unannounced, you blubbering fool?" roared the King, poking at the heaving mass with his cloven toe. "If you don't stop your noise and talk sense, you'll stoke fires till **Judgment Day**."

The young Devil sniveled and swallowed hard. Stoking was a menial job for any demon, let alone one who managed a farm on earth. "It's—it's my gypsy slave," he blurted, trying to keep his voice steady. "He's so strong he pulled my well from the ground and he wants to drag home a bundle of trees for firewood!"

"Well!" bellowed the King, when the wretched thing whimpered pitifully, unable to stifle his terror. "You'd better start at the beginning and tell me everything."

Now when the demon had told how he'd captured the gypsy and made him his slave, he ended, "What chance do I stand in my own house with such a fellow around?"

"None, unless you show more sense," shouted the King. "Not with a servant so much stronger, and smarter, than you!"

"B-but what can I do?" the Devil wailed, wringing his hands.

"Keep quiet, for now, while I think," bawled the King, pulling at his pointed black beard. For he was more disturbed by what he'd heard than he cared to admit, even to himself. A bargain was a bargain, and this one still had six and a half years to go. Besides, it was plain the foolish young creature was no match for the sly fellow. It would be bad if gossip got around that a mere gypsy had outwitted a Devil, even one banished from Hell at the time.

"There's just one thing to do," the Devil King said, at last. "You must kill your servant—this very night. And mind you don't bungle the job," he added, banging his fist on the table. "If you do, it will go hard with you, and all of us Devils as well."

The Devil fled from the angry King, and back at home, he slumped down by the fire. How could he hope to kill the gypsy, who twice over had proved his terrible strength? It wasn't until he reached for the poker to stir up the dying embers that the demon knew what to do. With this heavy iron, he could knock out anyone, even a gypsy with the strength of threescore and seven! Grinning with pleasure, the Master hid the poker under a sack, and awaited his servant's return.

But when the gypsy came back from the fields and noticed the poker missing from its accustomed place, he guessed well enough what was going on. He ate heartily of black bread and borsch (beet soup) and wiped his mouth on his sleeve. He'd best be off to bed, he said, if he was to be up betimes to weed onions.

The Devil, unable to conceal the smile on his lips or the gleam in his eye, smugly bid his servant a good night, and pleasant dreams. "They'll be pleasant, all right," the Master muttered when the gypsy entered the shed next the house.

On reaching his bunk, with the heap of straw that served him for a mattress, the gypsy made a tight roll of his old fur coat. And after he'd placed it on the straw, he crawled into a corner and bided his time.

Toward midnight, when he heard the tapping of his Master's hooves, the gypsy started to snortle and snore. And by the time the Devil, poker in hand, reached the bunk, he was breathing so heavily the rafters shook. Then wham—wham—and wham—again and again! Down came the poker on the rolled-up fur, until the Devil ached all over.

When the gypsy's snores suddenly stopped, the Devil exclaimed, "I've fixed him now! But here's a last blow for good measure."

With another WHAM that all but made the bunk fly apart, the Devil delivered a final smack. It was then the gypsy uttered an "Ooo—ahh!" that sounded as if he'd just awakened.

"W-w-what?" stammered the Devil, too scared to believe his own ears. "Whatever's the matter?"

"Oh, nothing—ooo—ahh," the servant said, yawning tremendously. "A flea must have nipped me." And with that, he pretended to sleep again, and commenced to snore, louder than before.

By now the Devil's knees all but gave way. His horns quivered with fear. And as for his tail, that dragged like a rag. How he got out of the shed, and back to the Devil King, he couldn't tell. But by the time he had reached the royal presence, he was completely undone. "Your M-M-Majesty," he stuttered. "The fellow was sleeping soundly when I clouted him first. But after I'd hit him again and again, and hard enough to kill ten men, he awoke. A flea must have nipped him, he said, and began snoring again."

The Devil King, who was visibly shaken, said promptly, "This fellow is dangerous to keep around. Besides, he's too strong and sly for the likes of you. Pay off his wages for the seven years. That's the agreement. Send him away at once—and good riddance."

Though he agreed to do as the King commanded, when he had tunneled his way back to earth, the young Devil began to think of the money he'd lose. "Even the first year isn't over yet," he reasoned. "It's all very well for the King to say, 'Pay him off.' But it's my money he's talking about—my loss." The longer he thought about it, the more unfair it seemed, for when it comes to money, a Devil hates to part with any of it.

Before reaching his door, the Devil had contrived a scheme whereby he could hold on to all of his money and at the same time rid himself of his slave. "I'm not so stupid as His Majesty thinks," he muttered, lifting the latch. And once inside, he shouted, "Hey, Gypsy, come here. I've got something to tell you."

"Well, what is it?" grunted the gypsy, glancing up from laying the fire on the hearth. From the look on his Master's face, he was up to no good.

"Things are so dull around here lately, I'd like to have a stamping match—between you and me," the Devil said with a crafty smile. "If you can stamp harder than I, I'll double your nest egg at the end of your seven years of service. But if I stamp harder," he added, gleefully rubbing his hands together, "you'll get nothing of what I owe you."

"Fair enough," the gypsy agreed, wondering how he'd outwit his Master this time. Much as the servant disliked the arrangement, there seemed nothing to do but accept it, and hope for the best.

The Devil, mightily pleased with himself, swaggered ahead of his slave to a big white stone in the meadow. "My turn's first, of course," the Master said with a smirk and leaped to the stone. "Are you ready to see me jump?"

"Ready," rumbled the gypsy calmly enough, in spite of desperate imaginings as to what he might expect. But he didn't have long to wait, for no sooner did the Devil start jumping up and down than sparks crackled and flashed around his hooves. And the more the sparks flew, the louder the Devil laughed. When he was done, though his cloven hooves were broken, he was triumphant. "There," he panted. He curled his tail jauntily over his back. His horns were erect. "See if you can improve that!"

"It won't be hard," snorted the gypsy. For when his hand accidentally touched the water flask at his belt, he knew how to fool the simpleton. "Anyone can stamp sparks out of a stone. But only I can squeeze out water—after I've wiped off your hoof marks."

"I—I don't believe it," the Devil snarled, stooping to rub his sore feet. At the same moment, the gypsy bent over the stone and pretended to wipe it—but really to puddle water from his flask about the base.

Then the gypsy quickly leaped to the stone and started to jump. And the faster his feet flew up and down, the more water spurted up from the ground and splattered into the Devil's gaping mouth and muddied his clothes.

The Devil blanched to the roots of his horns, his eyes bulged from his head. With a howl of terror that echoed across the countryside, he jumped into the tunnel to Hell.

"He s-stamped on a stone and water came out," the groveling creature groaned to the Devil King. "You can see for yourself. My clothes—my face—are all w-wet!"

"Get up, idiot," the Devil King roared, once he'd pieced together the terrible story. "This wouldn't have happened if you'd carried out my command. Go home at once—and mind what I say. Get rid of your servant *at whatever price*. And if you don't obey this time, you'll stoke three times as many fires as any demon in Hell!"

But despite the King's threat and his own fright, the stupid fellow hadn't learned his lesson. He still couldn't help thinking of that money he'd lose if he rid himself of the gypsy by paying him off for the seven years. And besides, by the time he'd reached the farm, he had thought of the hammer he could throw three leagues, which was better than any other demon could do. There was no doubt about it. His servant might be stronger, and able to jump and squeeze water from stones, but when it came to hammer-throwing, no gypsy in the world could surpass him.

Tingling with confidence, the Devil dragged out a hammer so heavy seven men couldn't lift it and yelled to his servant, "Hey, Gypsy, come here. Did you ever see a heavy hammer like this? Well, I challenge you to a contest. If you, with all your strength, can toss this hammer farther than I, I'll double your money. But if not—ha, ha," he added, more sure of himself every minute, "you'll get nothing at all."

The gypsy, who was considering a daring scheme, scratched his head as if in doubt. "Well, come on," taunted the Devil. "Do you dare accept my challenge, or are you backing out while there's time?"

"Oh, I accept," said the gypsy. "I was just thinking. Let's toss the hammer over yonder mountaintop. On the other side, I have two brothers, both of them blacksmiths. They could use a fine hammer like this. You can throw first," he said generously, when his Master gasped and tried to back off. "Then I'll take my turn."

"No, no, I took the first turn before," the Devil said hurriedly, wishing he had never mentioned the hammer.

Now when the Devil saw the gypsy, who couldn't have tipped the hammer an inch if he'd tried, spit on his palms and grasp the handle in both hands, he was more afraid than he'd ever been. And when his servant paused and shouted in a tremendous voice, "Hallo, brothers! Can you hear? I'm tossing over the mountain a magnificent hammer. Make ready to catch it when it gets there," the Devil shrieked.

"Stop!" the Devil yelled in a frenzy of fear. "Don't throw my hammer away. I need it myself."

"As you like, Master," the servant said, bending to hide his mirth. "Don't forget, you'll double my wages for this. And now I'd best get back to the onion bed."

But as his servant started away, the Devil, his horns quivering with rage, suddenly thought of something else—a whistling contest. That was it! No one had ever whistled better than he. Even a brute with such frightening strength couldn't outwhistle him. And so, swallowing his pride because of the money, he cried, "Come back, Gypsy. Let's try a whistling match, before you get to work."

"And the terms?" the gypsy asked, a sly gleam in his eye.

"Oh, the same as before," the Devil said airily, once more sure of himself. "If I whistle louder, you'll forfeit your wages. Of course, if you win, I'll double your pay."

"If that's how you want it," the servant replied, with a pitying look. "But in all fairness, I must warn that my whistle's so loud you'll be struck blind and deaf, once you hear it."

Though the Devil paled at the thought of adding a new misfortune to those already suffered at the gypsy's hands, the evil creature wasn't one to give up. Besides, the whistling contest was his only chance of holding on to his money. "I wouldn't want that," he replied cautiously. "But what can I do?"

"Oh, that's easy," said the gypsy. "While I'm whistling, you'd best blindfold your eyes, and stuff sheep's wool into your ears."

"But how'd I know you're not cheating, what with my ears plugged and all?" the Devil asked suspiciously.

"You needn't worry about that," declared the servant. "You see, I whistle so loudly that even the wool can't keep out the sound entirely."

Convinced at last, the Devil consented to tie a handkerchief over his eyes and stuff wool into his ears. "You can go first," he told his servant, thinking it safer, in case he tried any tricks.

But no sooner had the demon blindfolded his eyes than the gypsy clutched him by the tail. Then he grabbed up a heavy cudgel and beat his Master within an inch of his life. SLAP—BANG—WHAM, first on one ear, then the other, the terrible blows rained down thick and fast. In vain the Devil shrieked for mercy. The louder he howled, the faster the stick flew, the harder the gypsy pinched his tail.

Now how long slave beat master, no one knows today. But only when the ugly Devil lay screaming at the gypsy's feet did he surrender his notion of saving his money. "If you'll only stop, I—I'll—" shrieked the demon.

"You'll what?" bawled the gypsy, with a resounding whack.

"I'll triple your wages at the end of seven years," the Master whined.

"AND—?" roared the gypsy, smacking the Devil's shoulders so smartly he yelped with pain.

"I'll set you free now if you'll show mercy," the Devil wailed.

"You're getting the idea," laughed the gypsy, with a crack at his legs. "What else?"

"I'll—I'll go away and never bother you again," screamed the Wicked One.

"And that's a safe promise," the gypsy chortled with another blow. "Because if you don't fetch my money now, and let me go, there won't be any life left in your miserable carcass."

So saying, the gypsy tossed his cudgel to the ground. And the Devil, so weak he tottered on his bruised legs, paid three times the wages he had first agreed for the seven-year term. With horns that seemed to droop and tears in his eyes, the Master watched his slave race down the road, whistling merrily and swinging his bulging money-bag. He was free, off to the wide world once more, a song in his heart, fortune ahead.

And as for the Devil, shamed and humiliated, he slunk through the tunnel back into Hell. Every bone in his body ached. He was bruised and sore. Fooled by a sly gypsy, undone by his own greed, he still had to face the Devil King's wrath.

6

TSAR BORIS AND THE DEVIL KING
(Bulgaria)

Long, long ago, in the land of the Bulgars, Tsar Boris ruled with justice and good humor and a merriment uncommon among monarchs. Once the serious duties of running the kingdom were over, he rested each day in the vineyard behind the palace walls. There he sipped tea from his golden samovar, and watched with pride the dancing of his lovely daughter, the Princess Maritza.

But besides his daughter and the endless glasses of tea he drank, the vineyard provided other entertainment for the jolly old Tsar. For there, tucked under the leaves, was the enormous bottle that imprisoned his flea. So tiny was the creature, at first, that the Tsar's old eyes could scarcely follow its leapings from here to there. "But it will grow," the sailor who had brought the creature from beyond the Seven Seas said. "And when it does, your Majesty will laugh as he's never laughed before."

And Tsar Boris did. For one day he left a black dot in the bottle and the next, the dot was big as a mouse. "Ha," the Tsar cried in glee and slapped his thigh, "no one on earth ever had such a big flea!"

The very next day, when the Tsar peered at the bottle and saw that the mouse-sized flea had grown to the size of a cat, he laughed until tears coursed down his ruddy cheeks. "'Tis a magic flea," Boris declared to his Chamberlain and pointed to the short black fuzz that sprouted all over the hard shiny shell. "Whoever heard of a flea with fur?"

As the days came and went, the flea continued to grow and so did the handsome fur on its back. Never had Tsar Boris laughed so much. At last, however, when the flea reached the size of a calf, and its fat sides pressed the glass, he laughed no more. "It's either you or me," the Tsar said with regret, for he no longer fancied the glint in the creature's eye, or the mean throb of its upper lip. "You'll kill me if I don't kill you first, and it isn't as if you hadn't furnished fun."

Now after he'd done away with the flea, Tsar Boris had a marvelous idea, for never had he seen a finer black pelt. "One could guess a thousand years, and still not guess the creature that once wore this skin," he told his Chamberlain. "Alive, the flea made me laugh for days. Dead, it can make me laugh for years!"

So saying, the Tsar ordered his Chamberlain to have the hide hung outside, on the palace wall. "Then send messengers throughout the kingdom," he commanded, his face wrinkling with mirth. "Bid them announce the royal decree: 'Tsar Boris will offer in marriage the hand of his beautiful daughter, the Princess Maritza, to anyone, pauper or prince, who can name the origin of the pelt. The guessing shall start at noon, in three weeks and a day.' And who can say when it will end?" he added, with a wink. "As for my beloved daughter, she is quite safe. No one can ever guess the right answer."

Thus it came about that on the appointed day, at the appointed hour, the Tsar, in robes of state and with crown on head, swept to the vineyard with his ministers. With much to-do he sat on a stool placed close to the skin on the wall. "From here I'll listen to all that's said, listen and not be seen," he chuckled to his Chamberlain.

When the Tsar heard the first suitor say, "That hide, my friends, is the hide of a buffalo calf," he laughed until he ached.

When the second declared, "No, no, you're wrong. The pelt is black. It's the skin of a black ram. That's plain as the nose on your face," the Tsar held his sides in merriment.

"That's no ram's skin," a third contradicted. "Only a foal, as yet unborn, wears a coat such as that."

By this time King Boris was laughing so hard the jeweled crown rolled from his head. When his Chamberlain recovered the diadem and replaced it, it toppled again.

One day, after three and thirty had passed, and Tsar Boris had listened to guesses all the way from the skin of a goat to that of a water buffalo, he became aware of a silence beyond the wall. And before he could send his Chamberlain to learn the reason, a white-faced servant rushed to him. "Sire, Sire," the man gasped, his teeth chattering so he could scarcely speak. "A man in b-black walked from the Black Sea. When he glanced around fire flashed from his eyes. The others scattered in terror. Now he stands alone before the wall, his eyes on the s-skin, and—and—"

"A man in black, eh?" The Tsar, only half listening, chuckled and hitched his stool nearer the wall. "It may be amusing to hear what he has to say!"

"B-but, Sire, you don't understand," the servant persisted, plucking at the Tsar's sleeve. "The man yonder is the Devil King! I saw horns 'neath his hood, and a forked tail twitch under his cloak."

But the man might have saved his breath for all Tsar Boris cared. "Go away and don't bother me," he ordered testily and waved the fellow aside. "Neither Devil King nor all his minions can guess the riddle of yonder hide—not in a thousand years!"

The Tsar cupped his hand to his ear and opened his mouth, prepared to laugh at anything. But when a voice—sharper than steel, colder than ice—cut through the silence and said, "The skin on the wall is the skin of a flea," he was stunned.

Tsar Boris blanched to the roots of his hair. Then, shaking from head to foot, he gasped. "What have I done to my darling daughter, the light of both my eyes? The Devil King has guessed right and I have given my word."

Now the grief-stricken father, foolish and old though he was, was a tsar, and a man of honor at that. And though he loved his daughter more than life, he had a promise to keep. "Lead me to the audience chamber," he told his Chamberlain sadly. "Show the Devil King to the imperial presence at once."

What passed between the Tsar of the Bulgars and the Devil King in the audience room, no one knows to this day. But the wedding followed shortly and no one ever saw a stranger couple. The Princess Maritza, who wore a chaplet of pearls on her golden hair, drooped with sadness. Slim and pale as a lily she stood, not glancing at the bridegroom. Now and then she raised her lace handkerchief to dab at tears that welled in her eyes.

And as for the Devil King, he was ugly and old, with a cruel mouth and swarthy skin. His mocking eyes which glittered coldly as the diamonds in his crown never left the face of his wan bride. He held his forked tail gracefully over one arm and his black velvet tights fitted with elegance.

The wedding feast was of royal splendor, but the Princess, sad and aloof, sat at her husband's side, not seeing the golden goblets and plates or tasting the wines and foods. When at last the Chamberlain announced the royal procession to the sea, she swayed when she rose, tears dimmed her eyes.

At the head of the procession was Tsar Boris himself. White though his face and trembling his hands, he sat on his steed regally. Behind him rode soldiers with the imperial banners of crimson and gold. Musicians with cymbals and lutes, and dancers in rainbow robes, escorted the royal couple, followed by courtiers in silks and jewels.

At the water's edge the procession halted. The music and dancing ceased. The Tsar dismounted and held out his arms to his

daughter. "This is the final farewell," the Devil King said, his thin lips curling cruelly. "My palace lies yonder—threescore and seven fathoms under the sea. No man can find the place, nor shall any human see the face of the Princess Maritza again."

And then, before the father could embrace her a last time, the Devil King snatched Maritza's hand. Out into the tossing waves he dragged her. Just before they closed over her head, the Princess uttered a heart-rending cry, "Father, dear Father, save me!"

Back at the palace, Tsar Boris brooded alone in his chamber. He laughed no more, neither did he take his rest in the vineyard. For seven days and seven nights he sat in his chair and refused to eat, or see anyone. But on the seventh day he staggered to his feet and called for his Chamberlain. Though his eyes burned with fever in their hollow sockets, the monarch's voice was steady. "No one, least of all the Devil King, can accuse the Tsar of the Bulgars of breaking his word," he said proudly. "I have given my daughter to the Devil King in marriage, according to my promise, but I never said he could keep the Princess forever!"

Then the Tsar described a daring plan. "Go at once," he commanded. "Summon the aid of all who man boats—sailing vessels, pleasure craft, and even fishing smacks. Whatever floats on water must go forth to find my daughter. For surely, with aid of instrument or glass, one on the waves' surface can peer down deep, deep into the depths of the sea and catch some light, some glimmer from the windows of the Devil King's palace. And then, when we know where it is, we shall devise a way to rescue the Princess," the old man concluded, his voice breaking in spite of himself. "Gold, a whole treasure room of it, awaits the one who brings my daughter back."

The Tsar sank into his chair and covered his face. And after a time, when he said no more, the Chamberlain ventured an opinion. The search was futile, he said. Had His Highness not heard the Devil King say that his palace lay threescore and seven fathoms down— that no one should see the Princess Maritza again—that—

"Silence! Get out of my sight, old man. Carry out my command unless—" roared the Tsar in a terrible voice. "Unless you fancy the dungeon!"

Terrified, the Chamberlain fled. Before another three days ended, the Tsar saw ten thousand ships, both big and small, moving over the waves. They probed the depths with hook, line and pole, and scanned the surface beneath with powerful glass.

But as days came and went—and then weeks, and finally

months—and still no trace was found of the Devil's palace, the Tsar
lost hope. He drooped on his throne. Sorrow and remorse gnawed at
his heart. With tear-dimmed eyes he stared at the wall. "Our Little
Father laughs no more," the palace menservants said.

"Nor is he like to," said their wives and wiped their eyes. For
they loved their merry Tsar, and the Princess Maritza was like a
daughter.

One day, the despairing Tsar ordered that tapestries and hang-
ings be stripped from the walls. "Hang them with black. We are in
mourning," he declared. "No lights shall burn after dark. Throughout
the kingdom, there shall be no singing, no sounds of mirth. As the
Tsar sorrows, so shall his subjects," he concluded. "Any who disobey shall be chastised."

With the Tsar's decree, the land that once was joyous lapsed
into melancholy. No rustic gaiety ushered in spring, no feasting and
dancing accompanied the binding of autumn sheaves. Even at weddings there was no fiddling, no happy ceremonies marked the birth of
a child.

Everyone in the kingdom mourned with Tsar Boris—everyone,
that is, except the old woman with six handsome sons. All day long,
she sang merrily. And at night, when they trooped home from the
fields, her humble cottage blazed with light. Laughter poured from
the windows. The songs of happy youths roared through the night.

Now when the disobedience of the old woman came to the
ears of Tsar Boris he was exceedingly wroth. "Bring her here," he ordered, pounding the table with his fist. "I shall teach her to defy my
orders."

But when the old one stood in his presence and the Tsar saw
the contentment in her face, his mood softened. "Tell me, good
woman," he asked, leaning forward. "Why do you disobey my command? As you well know, since the Princess has gone, no one may
burn light, no one sing. Therefore, what is your reason for doing
both?"

"Most glorious Majesty," said the woman, bowing low. "So
long as you, my Tsar, and my six sons live, I shall rejoice in this life
so much that I must sing, even as the birds in the trees. My sons, who
are different from any other young men in the kingdom, are my pride
and joy. When they come home at night, they must have light . . .
music . . . fun."

"How are they different, I'd like to know?" the Tsar thundered, losing patience. "You'd better explain, old woman, before I
mete out the punishment you deserve."

"That, my Tsar, I shall gladly do," replied the mother, as she checked off the names of her sons on her gnarled fingers—from youngest to firstborn. "My sixth boy, Ivan, has such sharp ears he can put his head to the ground and hear anything in the whole world. My fifth, Simeon, has such a strong back he carries ten men easily as a goose-down pillow. When the fourth lad, Samuel, strikes his fist on the ground, a stone tower arises at once."

"But the third?" the Tsar cried, wild hope stirring in his breast.

"My third, Michael, is a fine marksman. An arrow from his bow hits anything—even a dot seven leagues away," the old woman boasted. "And my second son, Peter, is really unusual. He can breathe back the spirit of life into one who is dead."

"Aha," said the Tsar and pulled at his beard. "Well, go on, woman. What does your firstborn do?"

"My eldest son, Cyril, is most remarkable of all," the old one said, scarce able to contain her pride. "He drinks the ocean dry at a swallow."

"Ho," shouted the Tsar, leaping from the throne and embracing the old woman. "I can use men such as your sons. You have proved they are different from other youths. Send them here at once. If what you say is true, I promise you shall soon be even prouder and happier than now."

The old one lost no time in hurrying home and delivering the Tsar's message. And when her sons bowed before him, a short time later, the monarch thought he'd never seen such clear eyes or handsome faces. If anyone could wrest his daughter from the Devil, these stalwart young men of extraordinary prowess could perform the task. "If you can rescue my daughter and overcome the Devil King, your reward shall be as great as my gratitude," he said and turned to the eldest brother. "You, Cyril, shall wed the Princess Maritza, and be Tsar when I die. And as for the others, you shall be my ministers. Honor, riches and fame shall be yours."

"We shall not fail, your Majesty," said Cyril, bowing low. "We shall restore the Princess to your arms."

So saying, the brothers leaped from the palace.

Once the brothers had reached the shore of the Black Sea, the youngest, Ivan, laid his ear next the ground. "The Devil King's palace lies yonder," he said, listening intently. "I hear him breathing deeply. He sleeps so soundly he hears nothing, not even the Princess, weeping as though her heart would break."

"Then we must carry her away, while we can," cried Cyril, kneeling at the water's edge. He opened his mouth and drank so deeply that in one gulp he'd drained the sea dry. And lo! where only water had been the moment before, the palace of the Devil King now stood. Its coral pinnacles, blood-red and sharp, rose out of tangled seaweeds. Coal-black pearls studded the somber battlements. And there in the garden, surrounded by a wall of needle-pointed shells, and tentacles that writhed and throbbed, sat the Princess sobbing.

"She's crying her pretty eyes out," whispered Ivan, moved by compassion.

"And small wonder," Michael hissed, pointing to the open door of the palace. There, on a couch, lay the Devil King in exhausted sleep. Even in deep slumber, his ugly face contorted in rage. His forked tail twitched.

"Hurry," rumbled broad-shouldered Simeon. "We have far to go and no time to lose. Mount my back and hold fast. They've had a violent quarrel. We must carry the Princess to safety before the fiend wakens."

With his five brothers on his back, Simeon gave a mighty leap that carried him over the wall of shells, the tentacles that sucked toward his feet. The next instant, he stood panting beside the maiden.

"Hush, and fear not," Cyril whispered and slid from his brother's back. For the girl was terrified at the sight of one youth carrying five. "Your father, the Tsar, has sent us to bring you home. Come. I'll help you to my brother's back."

"It's no use. He'll kill me," said the Princess, sobbing harder than ever. "He said so—if I try to escape. Besides, he's furious. We had a terrible row, because I c-cry all the—"

"There's no time for tears. Get on my back, and be quick," Simeon ordered. "With us you have nothing to fear."

Cyril helped the Princess to Simeon's shoulders. Then, with his arm supporting her, the eldest brother whispered comforting words in her ear. And by the time Simeon had leaped across the writhing tentacles and was speeding toward the distant shore, Cyril was madly in love with the beautiful Maritza.

Just when the brothers thought themselves well on the way to getting the Princess home, a fearful uproar rose from behind. As if a hundred thousand creatures announced their escape, there were bellows and shrieks and a sea lion's roar.

"Quick, Brother Cyril," shouted Ivan, looking over his shoulder. "The Devil's pursuing us. He's close on our heels. Open your mouth. Pour back the sea."

Now when Cyril opened his mouth and the waters of the sea poured out, they lost sight of the Devil—for a moment. Then his leering face appeared on the waves. His dark arms struck out with powerful strokes. He swam toward the brothers with incredible speed.

"Stop, Simeon, stop!" yelled Cyril. "Brother Samuel, strike the ground with your fist. Only the tower can save us now."

No sooner had Samuel pounded on the bed of the sea than a tower of stone, with thick walls and a great iron door, shot into the air. And not a second too soon! For just as Cyril had whisked the Princess inside and the others had followed, and Michael had turned the iron key in the lock and fastened the iron bolts and chains, the Devil caught up with them. "Open the door, you fools," he screamed and pounded with all his might. "Give me back my bride or I'll come in and get her and string all of you up like crows on top of the tower."

"Well, why don't you?" Cyril taunted, rattling the chains. "You can't scare us, for we know that even the Devil can't pass through a door made of iron!"

The Devil snorted with rage, then a cunning glint came into his eyes, and he put on a show of grief intended to melt Maritza's heart. "Dear human bride," he sobbed. "If you only knew how much I love you, how lonely I am without your sweet presence, you'd not torture me thus."

But the Princess, trembling with terror, hid her face upon Cyril's shoulder. The Devil tried another tack. "Oh, you six brothers, have you no mercy in your cruel hearts? I promise to go away forever and let you take my poor bride where you will, in return for one small favor. Let me gaze upon the Princess Maritza's face, one last time. Surely that is not too much to ask," he concluded with a pitiful whine. "Let me, at least gaze upon the tip of one dear finger."

At first the brothers tried to ignore the Devil's pleadings. But when his moans and whines grew more insistent, the six decided to consider his proposal. "What shall we do? With the Devil outside, the Princess is in danger."

"And so are you," pointed out the girl.

"True. We can neither escape nor remain here forever," Simeon agreed, knitting his brows.

After they'd deliberated this way and that for three days, the Princess begged the brothers to allow her to stick the end of her little finger through the keyhole. "He won't leave until I do," she declared. "And with you standing behind me, should he try any tricks, what possible harm can he do?"

At last the youths agreed reluctantly to do as the Princess wished. "The Princess Maritza has decided to let you look upon her fingertip—if you leave her in peace and depart," Cyril shouted out to the Devil.

"I will, I will," whimpered the Devil. "I knew she'd not take this one joy from me."

But no sooner had the Princess poked her slender finger through the keyhole than the Devil King froze her, so that her breath left her body. And when she fell back unconscious into Cyril's arms, Satan howled with glee. "Stupid fools," he shouted. "That should teach you not to bargain with the Devil King! Now take the girl home, if you like," he mocked as he ran to the sea. "The Tsar will think you killed her and cut off your heads!"

With a triumphant shriek, the Devil King plunged into the waves and swam toward his palace. It was then that Michael, whose arrow never failed, snatched up his bow and raced to the top of the tower. And though the Devil was swimming so fast his head was only a black bobbing dot on the waves, the arrow hit it. With a blood-curdling scream, the demon vanished into the sea.

"The Devil King is overcome, his power gone," shouted Michael.

Peter, meanwhile, was bending above the still form of the Princess. And when he breathed back the spirit of life between her lips, the frozen blood began to course through her veins. Soon a faint flush tinged her pale cheeks. Her white lids fluttered and she opened her eyes and smiled at her rescuer. "The Princess Maritza is alive and well," Peter shouted.

And now, with the Devil King vanquished and the Princess restored, the happiness of the brothers knew no end. Cyril led Maritza from the tower, and the others followed with laughter and shouts. "Now climb on my back," Simeon ordered. "I'll run all the way back to the palace."

As they approached the shore, the old Tsar, watching anxiously from the balcony, beheld the youths bringing home the Princess in triumph. With exceeding joy he summoned his Chamberlain and all his court and ran to meet them. "My daughter, my little dove," he cried and held Maritza close. And when the Tsar had done kissing her lovely face, he embraced Cyril and each of his brothers in turn. "My son—and my ministers," he said. "Now I know why your mother sings all day. Her sons, her pride and joy, are different from other young men of the realm!"

Three weeks and a day from the time the brothers returned, the Princess and Cyril were wed. Wedding bells rang, and everyone in the land rejoiced in the happiness of the young couple. "Never did I think to have such a beautiful daughter, and a Princess as well," Cyril's mother said, gazing in rapture at the beautiful bride.

"Nor I such a merry son," chuckled the Tsar.

And now Tsar Boris laughed again. Once more he rested in his vineyard—when affairs of state were done—and drank tea from his golden samovar. But to the day of his death, he couldn't abide the sight of a flea!

7

THE SCHOOLMASTER
AND THE DEVIL
(England)

On a certain dark night, long ago, a dejected young Devil in search of souls hovered above the secluded hamlet of Cockerham— close to Morecambe Bay, on England's west coast. His black wings drooped wearily, for he'd flown far, and with no luck at all for all the effort. Catching sight of the old church tower, he decided to rest there and think over what to do next.

"Not that this is an ideal spot," he remarked, making sure his wings did not brush the cross. As he crouched on the parapet he glared balefully at the peaceful scene below. There were farms, rich fields of wheat, and the small stream—the Cocker—that flowed seaward, through a village of thatched cottages. In the wide bay, fishing craft bobbed. Waves lapped the sands, tides ebbed and flowed. And to add to his annoyance, the Devil saw happy children running about on the beach, shouting and laughing at a game of tag.

"Bah! Only farmers and fisherfolk," grumbled the Evil One. "Stupid oafs content with the same dull existence as their fathers and grandfathers, and their grandfathers' fathers before them! Even a very clever Devil like me doesn't stand a chance with the likes of them."

The Devil stared morosely at the overgrown graveyard directly below the tower. What with the singeing he got the last time he returned to Hell without prey, he didn't dare risk worse punishment. Still, no Devil alive could expect to get souls from such an unpromising place as this.

Or could he? All at once the Devil sat straighter and his tail switched excitedly. "Nothing's changed down there in a thousand years. From yon graveyard on the hill I can see everything that goes on, yet no one can see me. I'll make scary noises and frighten these folks half to death. And after I've upset their nerves and put things at sixes and sevens, they'll come crawling, begging for their dull life once more—on my terms."

With a joyous shriek, the demon swooped into the churchyard. And there, after poking his hooves at nettles and weeds, and sticking his nose behind crooked stones, he spied a flat moss-grown tomb. "Ha—a knight long dead lies here," he shrilled. With a nimble leap he

64

was up on the grave. He squinted his round saucer eyes to read the inscription:

> *Here lyeth Sir John that was as ye,*
> *And ye as he shall shortly be.*

The Devil rubbed his bony hands. "Well, I'll not be as ye, Sir John," he said gleefully. "But I'll shove over your dusty bones and crawl in beside you for a while. And when I return to Hell, it won't be alone," he added with a loud cackle. Before he vanished under the lid of Sir John's tomb, the Devil swept his eyes about the churchyard. Neither sickle nor scythe had touched the grass for months. "I can stay here as long as I like with no one the wiser," he laughed. "In Cockerham, nobody dies in less than a hundred years—and then he's soon forgotten!"

That very night strange goings-on disturbed the village. The trouble began with howlings and shrieks that startled folks from sleep. Then high winds arose, followed by zigzags of lightning, rumbles of thunder. While men ran to fasten shutters and slide rusty bolts, women rocked wailing little ones and sobbed, " 'Tis the Day of Judgment come in the night!"

Morning dawned calm, but the fishermen found their nets torn and the catches lost. And on the bay floated the wreckage of boats, washed from their moorings during the night. "Alas, we are ruined," cried the men, wringing their hands in despair. "Without boats or nets, what can we do?"

"The Evil One is in our midst," the young parson said, shaking his head, though at the time he didn't know how truly he spoke.

And all the while the Devil, puffed with wickedness, hid under the tombstone and schemed new miseries for the people of that village. "This is but the beginning," he chortled as he poked old Sir John's ribs with his own sharp elbow.

Night after night the Devil continued his bloodcurdling howls. Things went steadily from bad to worse. Cows strayed, horses broke legs, lambs were stillborn. And in the dairies, farmers' wives toiled in vain. Though they labored at the churn till their arms ached and sweat poured from their brows, no butter came. Pins dropped into wells, fennel in keyholes, and ashen-twig crosses over the doors did no good. Even the magic words,

> Come, butter, come,
> Peter stands inside the gate
> Waiting for his butter-cake.
> Come, butter, come,

that never failed their mothers and grandmothers, didn't help now!

On top of everything else, Satan caused a strange blight to fall upon first the rye, then the wheat. Only then did the people of Cockerham discover the awful truth. "A Devil's amongst us," they whispered, wringing their hands. "We must outwit him—but how?"

'Twas then the old ones spoke up. As children, they remembered their grandfathers tell of the Wise Woman of Pilling, a hamlet seven miles distant. She had routed a demon that all but destroyed the village. "She used magic," they said. "Let's go to the parson. Only he can help us. He'll exorcise our Devil with prayer."

Thus it was that a deputation, headed by the Mayor, visited the parson. But the Devil, unknown to anyone, had visited him first. They found the man of God delirious with fever, babbling strangely. "He can't help us now," the Mayor said, scratching his head. In the gloomy silence that followed, he suddenly shouted, "There's the schoolmaster! He has learning. He reads Latin and Greek—has ancient books on incantations and spells."

No one had ever thought of the bookish old man with bent shoulders and wispy hair—who stayed apart from village affairs— as one to help in such a crisis. "He'll know what to do," said one man. "He's taught our children well, these fifty-odd years."

When the citizens went to the schoolmaster's house and presented their problem, he was pleased. "Tell the villagers I shall not fail them," he said and sent the deputation away.

No school was held that day, or the next, or the one after that. The schoolmaster pulled the shutters and fastened the latch and got to work. He surrounded himself with parchments and volumes so huge the table creaked 'neath their weight. Hour after hour, without pause to eat or sleep, the old man pored over his books. And though he turned page after page on witchcraft and sorcery, he failed to find what he sought. "Yet there is a way to outwit a Devil, and find it I shall," he cried, as beads of perspiration gathered on his brow, and the letters danced before his weary eyes.

But all the while the schoolmaster bent over musty folios, the Devil howled without. He whistled over chimneys and shrieked through the deserted street. He rattled windows with bony hands until grown-ups trembled, children hid their heads in the bedclothes.

To the fearsome noises the learned man paid no heed. When one candle burned low, he kindled another. When one book was done, he took from the shelf one more dusty tome. And thus three days and three nights passed.

It wasn't until the third night waned, and the weary schoolmaster had turned the last page in the last tattered book, that the words he sought leaped at him: "If an evil spirit should bedevil and haunt thy village, do thou draw into a cup seven drops of thy blood. Then hie thee to the graveyard before dawn and alone and conjure up the Devil from his hiding place."

Further instructions and incantations followed. The old man read them with fast-beating heart. "Once the Devil stands before thee, the matter rests 'twixt thy wits and his. Think well, Brother. If thou canst name a task beyond his power, victory is thine. But if thou failest, thy soul is his. Therefore think well. In Heaven's name take care."

The schoolmaster closed the book and scraped back his stool. "Heaven will help me," he said resolutely. Now that the moment had come to test his learning, his heart thumped wildly, his hands shook. He opened the shutter and peered at the sky. The howlings had ceased. Stillness brooded over the hamlet. The moon hung bright and round. "There is yet time before dawn," he said. Then he pricked his finger and made ready the cup.

Moments later, on his way to the churchyard, the schoolmaster passed the blighted fields, separated one from the other by hawthorn hedges heavy with dew. "In the moonlight they sparkle like a hundred thousand diamonds," he said softly. Then he laughed. Seeing the dewdrops gave him an idea for the Devil's first task—a task that surely was beyond his power.

Clutching the cape about his thin shoulders, the old man crossed the noisy stream that hurried seaward, and pushed open the churchyard gate. "Woo—hoo," shrieked the owl in the yew tree, where black-winged bats flitted like vampires. The schoolmaster shivered in spite of himself. He took a firmer grip on the cup and advanced till he reached the middle of the burying ground. In a steady voice he repeated the charm to summon the Devil:

> Rise up, Fiend, rise up.
> Seven drops in a cup.
> Rise up, Devil.
> Reveal thy face.

No sooner had the schoolmaster spoken than smoke blinded his eyes, a thunderous roar deafened his ears. Something snatched the cup. And then the smoke cleared and there stood the Devil, saucer eyes blazing, horns aquiver with rage. "What brings you here, skinny old one?" bawled the Devil in a horrible voice. "I'll curdle your blood till you'll wish you'd stayed with your musty parchments."

"Well, will you now?" the schoolmaster asked coolly. With his success in conjuring up the Devil, new courage surged through his veins. Surely, a man of his learning needn't fear to match wits with anyone, even the Devil. "Then you'll have to prove it," he said. "For the villagers have sent me to bargain for peace."

"They have, have they? And what do they think such an old fool can do?" taunted the Devil, twitching his tail.

"Well, even you have to admit I've made a good beginning, forcing you to reveal yourself. Now I'll give you three tasks," the schoolmaster replied. "If you can do them—"

"You're mine!" chanted the Devil joyfully. His saucer eyes burned like lanterns. "I'll drag you to Hell like a sack of meal!"

"And if you can't," the old man reminded him, "you'll leave for Hell—alone—to sizzle forever in your own fires."

"If I can't!" mocked the Devil, holding his sides with laughter. "As if there's anything I can't do! Ha, ha! Well, have it your way, old bookworm. Only don't say I've not warned you. But hurry," he added, glancing at the moon. "We haven't all night. Name your first task. We'll be off soon."

"Count all the dewdrops on all the hawthorn hedges yonder," the schoolmaster replied promptly, his eyes gleaming behind his spectacles.

To his horror, the schoolmaster saw that the Evil One summoned a host of demons to his aid. Like black ugly beetles they skimmed up one hedgerow and down another. And as they flew, faster than eye could follow, they shrilled their count with awful exactness, "One thousand and one—three hundred thousand and thirty-three—four hundred million, two thousand threescore five." And all the while the Devil stood grinning—grinning and rubbing his hands.

In what seemed less than no time the Devil was back. "There are in all seventy-seven million, nine thousand and ninety-nine dewdrops," he announced with a smirk. "Now for your second task, old man, or has the cat got your tongue?"

When the schoolmaster, shaken by the failure of his first attempt to outwit the fiend, hesitated, the Devil roared, "Well? With all your learning, can't you think up something difficult?"

"Count the grains of wheat in yonder field," said the old man steadily enough, though his knees knocked together with fright. To number wheat grains was harder, surely, than to count drops of dew!

When the Devil sprang into the field, shouting, "Ha, ha, is *that* the best you can do? This task is easier than the first. Even young demons can count grains of wheat, unaided!" the schoolmaster's heart

plummeted to the soles of his boots. He watched with growing uneasiness as the Evil One stretched out his arms and cut down the
wheat, as by magic. He bundled the stalks into sheaves. And then,
after flailing them with his forked tail, he sat cross-legged in the
field and counted the grains.

"I must not fail the third time," groaned the schoolmaster
desperately, as the Devil neared the end of his second task. It wasn't
till he was counting the grains in the last handful of wheat, however, that the old man remembered something he'd read—something
no demon could do.

When the Devil bounded toward him bawling, "There are FIVE
BILLION, SEVEN TIMES SEVENTY TRILLION grains of wheat in yonder field,"
a smile twitched at the schoolmaster's lips. "Quick, quick, the third
task," the Evil One sneered. "If you have brains, bunglehead, I advise you to use them on your last chance. Of course, you're not much
to carry," he added, looking at his frail body. "But Hell's a right good
piece away. So hurry!"

But the schoolmaster didn't hurry, even though the Devil made
horrid faces and tapped with his hoof. His eyes, big as dinner plates
now, spluttered wickedly. The learned man, quite sure of himself,
wasn't afraid any more. "Fashion a rope from the sands on the
shore," he said deliberately, and nodded toward Morecambe Bay.
"Twist the strands well. Make them stout and strong enough to dip
and wash in the stream that flows outside the churchyard gate."

"Ah-ha, that I shall, though I really thought you smarter," cried
the Devil pityingly. "Watch me, doddering fool, and you'll discover—
too late—how stupid it is to try to match your wits with mine."

The Devil bowed mockingly. Then with incredible speed he
was off to the shore. Once more he summoned his imps. With lightning
swiftness their nimble fingers fashioned from sand a rope the like of
which no man had yet seen. When their work was done, the strands
were even and smooth, stout as though twisted from hemp.

The schoolmaster, meanwhile, waited beside the fast-flowing
Cocker, and while he waited he prayed, "Dear Heaven, help me," he
said, and made the sign of the cross.

Soon the schoolmaster heard a commotion. The demons were
coming in procession from the beach. Behind them they dragged the
rope of sand—heavy as lead, tawny as wheat. At their head capered
the Devil, grinning and rubbing his hands. "Hi, old man," he shouted
in glee. "Are you done with your prayers? Where we're going, you'll
need every one!"

When the imps reached the bank of the stream, the Devil ordered them to coil the rope round and round like a snake. Then waving them away, he knelt and lowered the end of the rope toward the water. "Watch this!" he shouted. "And be ready! It won't take long to show how easy it is to wash this rope in the stream."

"Then get on with it," said the schoolmaster dryly. "I'll be ready when you're done."

With a roar of triumph the Devil dropped the end of the rope into the flowing Cocker. But the instant the tightly twisted strands touched the water, they fell apart before his eyes. The more rope he uncoiled, the faster it dissolved, the quicker the current carried the sand to the sea. The Devil's roar of triumph turned to howls of despair, for no matter what he did, the rope crumbled. Bit by bit it vanished entirely.

At last the Devil, livid with rage and quaking with terror, turned on the schoolmaster. "You skinny pie-faced swindler," he bellowed. "This time you have outwitted me, thanks to the silly learning inside your skull."

"And the holy sign," said the schoolmaster.

At mention of the holy sign, the Devil uttered a wild shriek. He spread his leathery wings and flapped seaward. Blackness filled the sky. "And through the blackness we saw lightning," the farmers said, recounting the event, later.

"And heard thunder roll," attested some.

"And then a huge ball of fire shot out to sea," everyone agreed. "Angry waves reached toward the fearsome thing and sucked it down, down to the depths of Hell."

Now when the people saw and heard these happenings, they knew that their learned man had indeed foiled the Devil. Men, women and children ran out to meet him. "You have saved us and restored peace to our village," they cried, and grasped his hand in gratitude.

"Not I," replied the schoolmaster modestly. He gazed fondly at the children, who gathered around and tugged at his threadbare coat. " 'Twas not I, but the wisdom I found in books, together with God's help."

From the day the schoolmaster outwitted the Devil until now, no evil spirit dared visit the village again. Those who still tell the tale point with pride to the coast. "Yonder lie Cockerham Sands," they say. "That's where the stream deposited the strands of the Devil's stout rope."

8　THE GRATEFUL DEVIL
(Brazil)

Everyone loved the heir to the throne of Brazil, young Prince Martinho. For besides being the handsomest youth in all the world, he was pious and good. Even as a boy he hated injustice and brutality to weak and helpless things. If he saw a hunter setting cruel traps for animals, or a peasant beating his donkey, the wrongdoer had instant reason to quail before Prince Martinho's wrath. "When he succeeds his father he'll be a just King," the people said, nodding approval.

All the King's subjects, from greatest to least, took pride in their Prince. And as for his mother, the young Queen—he was her joy, her jewel, the apple of her eye. "My Martinho is destined for greatness," she always said.

As the years came and went, and Martinho grew from childhood into youth and waxed strong in body and mind, the Queen kept wondering what direction his greatness would take. Would he be a musician, a poet, or perhaps a sage—besides, of course, being the best ruler on earth?

The more the Queen pondered the question, the more she longed to ask a seer what he saw in Martinho's future. "Such a one could foretell our son's destiny," she told the King wistfully.

But the King, not caring to tempt Providence, always shook his head. "It's bad luck to pry into the future, my dear. God will reveal it in his own good time."

The Queen wasn't one to be put off, however, and after Martinho celebrated his eighteenth name day, she renewed her request. "*Please*, dear heart, now that our son's of age," she begged, "let me summon a soothsayer to the palace. I've heard of an old man whose predictions always come true."

The Queen's eager face was hard to resist. Unexpectedly, the King said, "If it will amuse you, call the fortune-teller." But no sooner had he given his consent than he was uneasy, for some reason he couldn't explain.

Three days later, when the old seer with a long dingy beard hobbled to the palace, the King felt even more uneasy. The soothsayer stared intently at the face of the Prince and then blanched.

"Your Majesties, I—I cannot foretell your son's fate," he mumbled and turned to leave.

The King, at first, was taken aback. Then he was furious. Watching the fortune-teller, he decided he was withholding the truth. "Come back," he commanded. "Reveal whatever it is you have seen."

The old man's voice trembled. "Sire," he said. "Your son, Prince Martinho, shall be condemned to die . . . on the gallows."

With a heartrending cry, the Prince's mother swooned at the dreadful declaration. Sorrow filled the palace. Later, the Queen insisted upon calling in another soothsayer—and then another. And when the prognostication was the same, each time, she gave herself up to grief.

For the young Prince, everything had changed. When his father thought no one was about, he sometimes heard him mutter, face in hands, "I said no good could come from prying into the future."

Martinho's mother wept night and day and refused to be consoled. "My son, my son, what have I done to you?" she sobbed, crying as though her heart would break.

"Nothing, dear Mother. What's to be will be," said Martinho sensibly. "In this life, only death is certain. Whether it comes sooner, or later, isn't important, so long as we are prepared."

The Queen wept harder than ever. "But one so young, so good—to be c-condemned—" she moaned.

"Hush, hush, who can say?" comforted Martinho. "If fate decrees I'm to dangle from a rope for what I've done, doubtless I'll deserve it. All the same, I intend to see I don't," he added more cheerfully than he felt.

All that night, Martinho tossed and turned. He kept wondering what he could do, to deserve the noose. It wasn't that he was afraid of dying. But with his parents grieving so much, he couldn't help wishing he could go away. It would save them pain, should he meet his fate at a distance.

Adventure—a journey! He'd tell his parents he wanted to take a journey, go adventuring. Suddenly Martinho sat up in bed, eyes sparkling, head swimming at thought of his plan. If he stayed home, his father would grow more sorrowful, his mother weep her eyes out. But were he to ride away on his horse, make his own way until destiny overtook him, they'd suffer less. He'd be less protected.

His decision made, Martinho fell back on the pillow with a contented sigh. The next moment he was asleep, a smile on his lips.

The following day, Martinho begged the King and Queen to grant permission for him to go into the world and seek his fortune.

"Pray, give me your blessing, dear Father and Mother," he ended and added, with a lightness that didn't deceive his father, "Who knows—this way, I may even escape my fate?"

The Queen wept. With knitted brow, the King pulled at his beard. He suspected the real reason for Martinho's request. Yet if this was what he wanted, what right did they have to interfere? He, his father, would see that the boy took plenty of gold.

At last the King spoke. "Go, dear son, with our blessing and prayers and this gold," he said, and pressed a leather pouch into Martinho's hands. "Wear this inside your shirt. And remember, gold wisely spent brings happiness."

Martinho thanked his father. With tears in his eyes, he bid farewell to his father and mother. Then he leaped into the saddle of his dappled gray horse and galloped away to the north. Beyond the grassy plains, the broken mountains, lay another country. "That's where we'll seek adventure," said the Prince, patting his steed's sleek neck. "We'll live each day and leave the future to God."

After they'd journeyed seven days and seven nights across the broad plains and sparkling rivers of his father's kingdom, the Prince and his horse reached the mountains. Though the way was dangerous, and wild beasts roared from within caves and behind rocks, they made the journey without harm. At last they descended a steep winding slope, and entered a desolate village.

Martinho gazed about curiously. The few people he saw were apathetic and sad. The thatch on their roofs was old and torn, their huts sagged. Misery brooded over the village.

"Tell me, good Mother, what has happened?" the Prince asked, reining in his horse beside an old woman who carried faggots.

"What's happened?" cackled the crone bitterly. "We're poor and our patron, Sant' António—Saint Anthony—has forgotten us, that's what's happened!"

"Nonsense," Martinho said. "Sant' António sold his goods to help the poor. He doesn't forget them."

But the woman hobbled away and Martinho, more puzzled than before, rode on to a cobbled square. There stood a ruined chapel—with crumbling walls and crooked cross—dedicated to the patron Saint. "I'll stop here and give thanks for our safe journey," the Prince said. "God protected Sant' António from wild beasts in the wilderness—as he did us."

As Martinho tethered his horse, an aged man said, "Our chapel, alas, is falling to ruin. This village is poor. For what with drought and bad crops—then sickness that cost many lives, including our priest's—we've had no money, nor strength, to rebuild our sanctuary." He sighed deeply and concluded, "Even the statues of our saints are shabby. We've neglected Sant' António. Now he neglects us."

When Martinho entered the chapel, he had to admit the man spoke truly. The villagers had neglected their patron and the other Holy Ones, whose gold halos and brilliant robes once glowed like jewels from the gray stone walls. Now the halos were blackened, the painted faces peeling. Garments once scarlet or green or blue were faded and drab.

Most dismal of all was the figure of Sant' António. His long black robes were dingy with dust, the noble features scarred. The T-shaped staff had dropped from his fingers. And as for the Devil who'd tried to tempt the Saint in the wilderness with silver, then gold, finally a woman—his statue had fallen from the niche. Now the Devil—the symbol of evil that goodness conquered—rolled in dust, forked tail broken, cloven grooves nicked. Even the horns on the wicked head were splintered and dull.

"My, the villagers are careless," the Prince murmured, gazing about. In spite of grinding poverty, crop failures, sickness, the chapel was unbelievably neglected. These people had no initiative, they'd done nothing for themselves.

Deeply depressed, Martinho sank to his knees on the dusty stones and gave thanks for the safe journey across the mountain. When his hand accidentally brushed the pouch next his bosom, it gave him an idea that might change everything.

"What wiser way to use dear Father's gift than to help these people—get food to them, medical aid, find a new priest?" Martinho cried, springing to his feet. "Then I'll rebuild their chapel—with help from all who can work. I'll restore the statues to their former glory," he planned eagerly. The King had been generous. There was more than enough gold.

When Martinho hurried from the chapel and called the villagers together, his face was shining. And when he'd revealed that he, a Prince from a neighboring country, wanted to help them get on their feet along with repairing their chapel, they shouted with joy. "With your aid, dear Prince," promised the old man, speaking for all, "Sant' António won't forget us again, nor we neglect him."

By the time work on the chapel began, the people were stronger. Hope stirred the village. Each day, as the tumult of chisels on stone and mallets on wood increased, so did the excitement of the villagers. At last, everyone who could, from the oldest man to the youngest child, tried to help. Each did his part, from clearing rubble to fetching a stick or a stone. And Martinho was everywhere, busier and happier than anyone.

After many weeks and months, the head workman bowed before the Prince. "Master, our work is done," he said. "Pray come and inspect everything."

And this Martinho did, from the shining cross on the top to the new stones in the floor. "Come storm or wind, this sanctuary can stand a thousand years," he said, pleased with everything. Then he inspected the statues that adorned the walls.

When the Prince saw the gleaming halos, the pure purples and reds and greens of the enameled robes, the repaired hands and feet, he was even more pleased. And when at last he reached the image of Sant' António, he was beaming. Now the lips smiled benignly, the robes were immaculate. The delicate fingers held the staff high in blessing. "Perfect, perfect," murmured the Prince and complimented the head workman.

But suddenly Martinho's brow darkened. For his eyes, sweeping the niche, saw the figure of the Devil, kicked aside, shabby and broken as before. "What is the meaning of this?" he thundered. "You called your work done. Yet this image is untouched."

"B-but that is the D-Devil!" stammered the man, blanching. "I-I didn't know—"

"You do now," Martinho retorted. "Devil or not, restore the image. Mend it. Paint it. Make it elegant as the rest."

Only when the workmen had carried out his orders and the statue of the Devil, with mended tail and shining horns, again stood in its place near the Saint, did Martinho take leave of the villagers. "I have tarried long," he told them. "Your new priest comes soon. My horse and I must go."

"Thank you, thank you, dear Prince," cried the inhabitants, crowding around. "You have given back our saints, our church—our will to live," they cried.

As Martinho started down the long road his heart glowed with happiness. He gave no thought to the soothsayer's prediction. "Who knows what we'll do next?" he said, patting his horse.

The distance to the next town was greater than the Prince supposed. It wasn't until dusk of the third day that he saw a spire in the distance and smoke rising from chimneys. "Soon you'll get oats and fresh straw, my friend," he encouraged his steed. "Tonight, your Master will sleep in a bed."

On entering the town, Martinho soon found the only inn. The old woman who kept it had mean eyes and a knot of wispy gray hair on her head. Though he didn't fancy the crone's looks, the hour was late, his horse weary. "Pray bed down my steed, good woman," said the Prince. "Then show me my room."

Now when the innkeeper, who was miserly and dishonest, saw her lodger's fine cloak and heard his gentle speech, her eyes glittered with greed. "If it's money he's got, I mean to have it!" she muttered as she led the horse to the shed. Then she skimped on the feed the young man ordered and returned to the house.

The woman lighted a candle and took her lodger to his room. After bidding him a curt good night and closing the door, she loitered outside. She soon discovered that, by stooping down and peering through a knothole, she could spy on everything he did. When the crone saw Martinho remove a pouch from his neck, she pressed her eye closer to the knothole. When he dumped the contents on the table before him, she stifled a cry. Never had she seen such wealth. Thirteen bright gleaming pieces of gold, each worth a fortune!

By the time the woman had seen Martinho count the gold and return it to the pouch, her eyes bulged with envy. When he blew out the candle and climbed into bed, she'd devised an evil scheme that would profit her, at her lodger's expense.

On hearing the Prince's regular breathing, the innkeeper tiptoed to the mantlepiece and took down the silver candlestick her grandmother had left her. Then she crept back to her lodger's door. Inch by inch, she opened it. She entered the room stealthily, and placed the candlestick under the bed.

"That ought to fix the fool!" the woman gloated and hurried to the Mayor's house. She was reasonably prosperous, well thought of in the town. He'd believe her story.

At the Mayor's house, the windows were dark and he was in bed. "Help! Help!" the woman cried loudly and pounded on the door. "I've been robbed! Come quickly. When I turned my back, my lodger stole my life savings, the silver candlestick my grandmother left me."

When the Mayor heard the innkeeper's false tale, he quivered with rage. "Wait till I lay hands on the rascal," he sputtered. "I'll teach him to rob hard-working widows!"

All the way to her house, the old woman blubbered, "You'll see I'm telling the truth. You'll find my lodger asleep with my thirteen p-pieces of gold, my candlestick."

When the Mayor found that Martinho indeed had the gold

and the candlestick in his possession, he handed them to the old woman. Then he dragged the Prince from bed. In spite of his protests of innocence, the Mayor roared, "Scoundrel! I'm taking you to the Judge. You'll soon learn it doesn't pay to rob honest hard-working folk in this town!"

The Mayor delivered Martinho to the Judge, who found him guilty and called a guard. "Take him to jail," the Judge ordered. "As for you, young man, you'd best take the rest of the night to repent your crime. Come dawn, you'll hang at the end of a rope."

At the very moment the Judge condemned Martinho to death, Sant' António, in his chapel, turned to the Devil and asked kindly, "Now that your tail's mended, your hooves shine, and you're altogether as handsome as the rest of us, how do you feel, my friend?"

"Superb," cried the Devil. "Better than for two hundred years." In the glint of moonlight from the east window, he stretched out an arm to admire the shining surface.

"Do you know who's responsible for the elegant appearance you enjoy?" the Saint asked.

"N-no," replied the Devil, scratching his head. "Though I remember someone said 'twas a Prince from beyond the mountains, riding through the hamlet on a gray dappled horse."

"And so it was, Prince Martinho of Brazil, the handsomest, the most generous, the kindest young man in the world," Sant' António said and added, "He restored this chapel and all the statues. Were it not for him, your head would still be rolling in dust. You'd be shabby and forgotten. When the Prince discovered the workmen's neglect, he was furious. He ordered them to repair you, from the tip of your horns to the fork in your tail and to spare no pains in making you handsome." The Saint paused. Sighing deeply, he concluded, "Now, alas, the noble Prince is in trouble. He languishes in prison, falsely accused of robbing an old woman. She took his gold and he'll die on the gallows at dawn, unless—"

"Die on the gallows, eh?" snorted the Devil, his eyes flaring. "The Prince who rescued me?" His forked tail switched. "He'd not die—not if I were free to go—"

"GO!" thundered Sant' António, lifting his staff. "You have my permission. Save our Prince, then—"

The Devil waited to hear no more. He leaped to the door. Outside in the square, he clapped his hands. Instantly, a black steed appeared. The Devil, clothed in a black-hooded cloak, sprang to the saddle and turned the horse toward the next town.

As the horse galloped over the road like the wind, sparks flew from his hooves, fiery darts from his nose. The full moon was beginning to wane as horse and rider turned in at the gate of the inn. The Devil slipped from the saddle and led his steed to the shed, where he found Martinho's dappled gray. The creature neighed and pawed at the ground so furiously that the Devil stooped to examine it. When he found a human bone, his eyes burned dangerously, his tail switched.

"Ha, it took you, my beauty, to discover that the innkeeper murders, as well as robs," the Devil grunted, and stuffed the bone into his pocket. He raced back to the house and peered through the window. When he saw the crone hunched on a stool before the fire, counting her ill-gotten gold pieces over and over, he rubbed his hands in glee.

"Seven and three—and THREE—make THIRTEEN," the old one cackled and bobbed her head till her wispy topknot shook. "Tomorrow, when my lodger's dead, I'll buy me a silk gown, a gold brooch for my shawl and a ring—"

"Oh, no you won't," bawled the Devil, bursting in through the door. "Tomorrow you'll get a surprise. Tonight you'll confess your crimes to the Judge. And I'll take that stolen gold."

"No, no, I won't confess," screamed the old woman, trembling with terror at sight of the hooded stranger. "I'll not go to the Judge nor give up the gold."

"Or confess to the murder of travelers, I suppose?" the Man in Black mocked, shaking the bone under the crone's nose. With a chilling laugh he swept the coins into his pocket. "I'll return these to their owner. And since you're so loath to go to the Judge yourself, I'll help you!"

The next thing the woman knew, a dreadful claw hand grasped the topknot on her head. More dead than alive, she felt herself jerked through the streets. Her screams and kicks, her pleas for mercy, fell on deaf ears. Before she knew she was there, the Man in Black tossed her like a sack of potatoes through the door of the Judge's house. "Here's the real robber—and a murderess, as well," bellowed the Devil. Tossing the human bone after the woman, he disappeared.

The first rays of dawn were streaking the sky when the Devil reached the cell where Martinho, on his knees, prepared to meet death. The guard at the door was snoring. It was easy to slip the keys from his fingers and unlock the door.

Watching the guard from the shadows, the Devil's eyes glowed

warmly. "Psst!" he hissed. "Kind Prince, listen! You are free, the door is unlocked. Leave this town at once. Your horse awaits you at the evil old woman's. Hurry. You have no time to lose."

Before the astonished Prince could thank his rescuer, or even see him, the Devil tossed the gold at his feet and vanished.

The day was far spent and many miles lay between Martinho and the town where he had been condemned to die. Suddenly, he was aware of pounding hoofbeats from somewhere behind. When he turned in the saddle, he was surprised to see a black-hooded rider on a black horse, trying to overtake him. The Prince was even more surprised when the stranger reined in and addressed him by name. "Greetings, Prince Martinho," he said. "Where are you going?"

"In search of adventure wherever the road may lead," replied Martinho and added, "But tell me, how do you know my name? We've never met."

"Oh, yes, we have, twice." The hooded stranger laughed softly, as if enjoying a secret joke. "Didn't you wonder who released you from prison?" he asked.

"Indeed, yes," replied the Prince. "And I'd like to thank him for saving my life." He stared intently at the shadowed face. "Was it you?" he asked at last.

"Yes, it was!" cried the Devil and threw back his hood. The Prince gasped in astonishment. "I'm the statue of the shabby Devil you rescued from the dust. When Sant' António told me of your plight—and I learned who you were—I wanted to rescue you. The Saint bid me go, and now you're free. And as for the old woman—" The Devil paused, his eyes glittering wickedly. "At this minute, she's roasting in Hell. This was not her first crime. As it came out, she was guilty of many others against hapless travelers who stopped at her inn. She confessed to the Judge and died at dawn on the gallows in your place." The Devil chortled. "I switched your fate to her!" he added.

"You WHAT?" shouted Martinho, almost falling from his horse

The Devil paid no attention. "Go home to your grieving parents," he advised. "They need you, and so do your people. To the end of your days, kind Prince, you'll have nothing to fear."

When the Prince opened his mouth, the Devil had vanished.

Some weeks later, after Martinho had crossed the mountains safely and arrived at the palace alive and well, the happiness of the King and Queen was great. And when the Prince related his remarkable adventure, and told how the Devil had changed his fate, the whole kingdom rejoiced. And at the height of the festivities in honor of the Prince's safe return, he said, "You were right, dear Father, gold wisely spent does bring happiness."

"And gratitude—" mused the King, stroking his beard, "from even a Devil!"

9

THE THREE CLEVER
BROTHERS
(Netherlands)

There were once three clever brothers—Pieter, Ebbel and Jans —who lived in the poor Frisian village of Haulerwyk, in the north of the Netherlands. Their parents had died when the lads were young, leaving them penniless. Keeping body and soul together, and a roof over their heads, hadn't been easy. Still, with courage and plenty of hard work, they managed well enough.

The brothers took on any jobs that came to hand, from digging ditches to hauling stones. Yet most of the time their stomachs yawned like empty sacks, and their pantaloons, though clean, were frayed and patched. What with hard times in the village and money scarce, the three never had a copper to spare. And as years passed, and things were worse instead of better, the lads, who had brains as well as brawn, often wondered how they'd get ahead in the world.

One night, after they'd supped scantily on thin soup and coarse bread, the eldest brother pushed back his stool. "What was good enough for our father and his grandfather's father isn't good enough for me," he sighed. "I could do wonderful things with money."

"Ha, and so could I if wishes were fishes!" muttered the middle brother, Ebbel, noisily scraping his spoon round his empty bowl.

Meanwhile, the youngest brother, Jans, scarcely more than a boy with the first fuzz on his face, swept his eyes over the mean room, the crumbling hearth, the patched hole in the wall. "Well, why don't we do something, then? Leave this wretched hovel, make a new start, and get rich?" he asked impatiently.

"Why not indeed?" mocked a voice from the door.

The brothers whirled about. When they saw the tall stranger in black standing there, his eyes glowing with uncanny light, they shuddered in spite of themselves.

"Who are you?" faltered Jans, trying to keep his voice steady. "What do you want here?"

"Oh, don't be alarmed." The stranger waved a hand airily. "I've come a considerable distance to help you. Tell me, young gentlemen, do you have any wishes?"

"Wishes," shouted Pieter angrily. "Anyone can see we have nothing else. All we need is money to carry them out."

"There's money enough," the stranger remarked quietly and advanced a step.

"Yes, and the Devil has it," snapped Pieter, pounding his fist on the table till the empty bowls jumped.

The stranger laughed softly and threw back his cloak.

"Then you are the Devil!" Jans gasped, recoiling in horror. For when the three saw the close-fitting tights, the long tail with the fork at the end, and the cloven hooves, they knew for certain who the man in black was!

While the brothers were still too frightened to speak, the Devil said in a voice smooth as silk, "I'll grant each of you your fondest wish, and ask no payment now. But after you've enjoyed yourselves, it will be *my* turn," he added, his eyes glowing brighter. "I'll come back, at a time we'll agree upon, and collect your souls, unless—"

"Unless—?" whispered Ebbel.

"Unless you name a task I can't do—which isn't likely," the Devil replied with a flick of his tail. "But if you can, you'll be free. I'll have no further hold on you and you'll never see me again."

In the stunned silence that followed, each brother heard his heart thumping wildly. Each one thought, here was his chance to get on in the world, to make something of himself, to have riches, fame. And yet—

Suddenly, as if in answer to the uneasiness all felt, Pieter boomed, "Buy now, pay later. That's your bargain, eh? Well, brothers, shall we accept or not? If we do, we all know that the Devil's bill lies at the bottom of the bag. The day of reckoning will come."

"And I want to know when that will be," Ebbel demanded, half-rising from his place at the table.

"The day of reckoning. Ah, yes." The Devil rubbed his hands with relish as he scanned the anxious faces. "Would you agree 'twould be fair for me to claim my reward when each of you reaches his threescore-tenth birthday? That way, you'd have had your fun," he added with a leer, "and plenty of time to—"

"Think up a task you can't do," cried Pieter, his blue eyes like ice. He had his own notions about dealing with the Devil. "I, for one, agree to your terms."

"So do I," Ebbel shouted, thinking of all he could do with his wish.

"Count me in," said Jans, his eyes sparkling as he stroked the fuzz on his face. To the youngest the age of threescore and ten seemed remote as Paradise.

"Well then, gentlemen, since we're agreed on terms, let's get on with your wishes," the Devil said cordially. "To carry them out by dawn, my demons and I shall have plenty of work," he added.

Then, from the eldest to the youngest, the Devil asked the brothers to name their wishes.

"This is my wish," said Pieter solemnly. "I want a mill for grinding rye into meal, to make the best bread our women ever baked. And I want to grow rich from it."

"So be it," the Devil said and bowed in mock deference. "Tomorrow at dawn go to the pond at the edge of the village. There you will see your mill." With an impatient switch of his tail, he turned to the middle brother. "And your wish?" he asked.

Without an instant's hesitation, Ebbel cried, "I also want a mill, not for grinding rye, but for sawing wood. I want to be able to slice forest trees into planks and boards, to make tables and chairs, and bridal chests carved with hearts and flowers. I want to saw timbers for houses and ships, and have money and fame."

"You shall have your wish," said the Devil, bowing again. "When you waken tomorrow, stay here. Before your eyes you shall see this hovel transformed into your mill."

The Devil had scarcely finished before Jans burst out passionately, "Let the others have their mills for grinding rye and sawing wood, but give me a ship. I want to be captain of a vessel that bounds over the waves, with billowing sails white as a seabird's breast. From Amsterdam to the Cape, and back again, I'd sail with ivories and gold and diamonds fit for a queen. Free and rich, I'd sail the Seven Seas, circle the earth three thousand times—"

The Devil raised his hand. "Go to the harbor at dawn," he said, stemming Jans' torrent of words. "There you'll find a sailing ship, awaiting her Master's command."

So speaking, the Devil swept off his hat. For the first time, the brothers saw the large pointed ears, the horns, and the round wicked eyes unshadowed by the brim. They moved uneasily as he smiled and said, "Good-bye, gentlemen, for now, and good luck. Your wishes shall be granted. When next we meet, you'll be weary and old— glad of the warm welcome that awaits you in Hell!" Then, in a stench of sulphur and splutter of sparks, the Evil One vanished.

What happened next, or how long they slept, if indeed they did sleep, the brothers never knew. When Pieter opened his eyes, gray light touched the sky. "It's dawn! Get up! Hurry!" he shouted and shook Jans and Ebbel, as the strange events of the previous night flashed to mind—the awful bargain with the Devil, the promise of riches, fulfillment of their wishes and dreams.

Was it all a dream? No! It was all real enough, for when the brothers wakened they were still in the hovel, and there was a pile of clothes for each. They sprang to their feet and dressed themselves in the garments. Everything fitted them exactly, even to Jans' gold-braided captain's uniform, with the sharp sword at the belt. When the three had pulled on their fine boots, fastened the last silver button, and slipped into their pockets the gentlemen's gold watches on heavy gold chains, they bid each other farewell. Then Pieter and Jans ran in opposite directions through the streets of the sleeping hamlet, while Ebbel remained where he was.

When Pieter reached the pond at the far end of the village, he gasped in astonishment. There beside the water, where yesterday there was nothing save sedges and reeds and black-and-white lapwings screaming, now rose a windmill, with sails that swept around and around with slow stateliness. Pride swelled Pieter's heart. "My mill," he murmured, clasping his hands. "The mill that will grind the finest rye meal in Friesland."

While Pieter was admiring his mill and poking at the well-filled sacks of rye inside, Ebbel watched the mean hut where he and his brothers had lived change as by magic into a vast lumberyard. Saws buzzed. Oak timbers and planks of birch and pine stood in neat piles. "My dream," Ebbel cried. "May all who fashion theirs from these woods, be happy as I."

And as for young Jans, when he raced to the habor and found a great ship awaiting her captain, he rejoiced exceedingly. She was his to sail to the ends of the earth.

For the brothers, whose fondest wishes had come true, the years that followed flew as on bird wings. In his own way, each achieved fame—Pieter as a miller, whose rye flour made the sweetest bread man ever tasted; Ebbel for woods that built humble homes and patrician mansions; Jans as the canniest captain on the Seven Seas. Each of the three had realized his dream. Each was rich. Yet with all their prosperity, they were generous. They helped other youths who had dreams.

As the years came and went, the eldest brother, Pieter, grew uneasy at last. For his hair, once shining gold, had turned to white. A stout cane supported his once springing steps. As his seventieth birthday drew nearer, Pieter was troubled, though not discouraged. "There's more than one way to skin a cat and more than one to outwit the Devil," he said. "All I have to do is find it!"

And Pieter did, or so he thought, on the eve of his birthday.

For three weeks and a day he had pondered the question, a frown on his face. Then suddenly the frown vanished, his great laugh shook the rafters. He lighted a candle and went to bed. When he pulled on his nightcap and tucked in the covers, he slept like a baby, though a crafty smile wrinkled his old face.

Day dawned bright and clear. Pieter leaped from bed and threw open the shutters. Peering first at the sky, and then toward the pond and the mill sails turning briskly in a wind from the sea, the old man muttered happily, "There never was a finer day to stay on earth!"

Pieter pulled his Sunday clothes from the chest and reached for his cane. When he arrived at the mill, the Devil was waiting. "Well, I thought you had forgotten our appointment," he said, tapping an impatient hoof. "Though, of course, at threescore and ten, you have to expect a man to be late," he added. "Happy birthday, anyway. What a party I've planned when we get to Hell!"

"You're kindness itself," Pieter said, with a low bow. "I'd hardly forget an appointment with you. If I'm late, it's because the occasion calls for festive attire. But haven't you forgotten that before we go, I'm entitled to give you a task?"

"Ah, yes, a task," the Devil said, with a snap of his tail. "There's nothing, of course, I can't do, though I'll not deny you the pleasure of trying me. But hurry, old man," he added, his round eyes glowing.

"Well then, here's your task," said Pieter with great show of haste. For an instant his eyes rested on the bulging sacks of meal, stacked to the roof of the mill. "You are to change the contents of these bags into grain, plant yonder field, and make the stalks of rye grow straight and tall as before the farmer cut them."

"You—you swindler!" the devil shrieked, shaking from horns to tail with terror and rage. "The task you propose isn't Devil's work. Devils ruin, destroy, tear down. Only God makes things grow!" Gnashing his teeth and stamping his cloven hooves till the windmill rocked, he pointed a trembling finger at Pieter and yelled, "I'm undone and you're free!"

With a howl that was more like a wail, the Devil vanished into the earth in a billow of black smoke. Pieter watched till it cleared, and he could see a patch of blue sky big enough to make a pair of Dutchman's breeches. Then he laughed till his sides ached and tears ran down his furrowed cheeks. When able to speak, he cried, "There is more than one way to outwit the Devil!" and patted his plump sacks with loving hands.

Once more the years passed and the second brother, Ebbel, began to think of his approaching fateful birthday. And though his step had slowed and his back was stooped, life was rich. He had a loving wife, children and grandchildren, and a house full of laughter. Ebbel had no notion of leaving them yet. Day and night he'd been considering a scheme that couldn't fail.

On the eve of his birthday, Ebbel woke to hear his wife sobbing. "Never fear, dear love," he comforted her. "Young men may die, old ones must. When my time is up and the Angel beckons, I'll follow. But I'll not let the Devil drag me away if I can help it."

Ebbel chuckled comfortably. And though his wife wheedled and wept, wild horses couldn't pull more from his lips. "I need my sleep," was all he'd say.

In the morning Ebbel twirled his stick gaily as he set out for work. His step was jaunty and his eyes twinkled. Arriving at the lumber mill, he sniffed at the scent of newly cut wood, passed his hand over the smooth boards of chestnut and beech.

Ebbel didn't hear the quick click of hooves from behind. He was startled when the Devil's voice rasped, "Happy birthday, old man. Are you bidding good-bye to your saws and boards? It's just as well, I suppose. It's my turn now, and I'm here to fetch you."

The Devil reached for Ebbel's arm, but the old man stepped out of reach. "Not so fast," he roared. "I have a task for you."

"Well, you'd better hurry then—and no tricks," snarled the Devil, for he smarted still from the thrashing he'd received on returning to Hell without Pieter's soul.

"No tricks but you'd better take care," Ebbel warned, so mockingly the Devil couldn't help a nervous twitch in his tail.
"Here's what you're to do," Ebbel went on, waving toward the stacks of lumber. "You're to turn all these planks and timbers back into trees, plant them in the forest again, and make them flourish as before I cut them down."

Ebbel watched the Devil's face turn sickly green and his body shake. "Rascal—cheat!" he shrilled. "What you propose isn't Devil's work. As you well know, God alone makes trees! And now you're free, while I—" He ended on a terrified screech, and his round eyes bulged from his head. Then earth opened up with a belch of smoke, and the Devil uttered a despairing wail.

When the smoke cleared, the Devil had vanished. Ebbel let out a loud guffaw.

Then he snatched up his stick and jammed on his hat and hurried home to celebrate his threescore-tenth birthday with his wife.

Again time passed, all too quickly for Captain Jans. One night, while sailing his clipper in the North China Sea, he suddenly remembered the Devil. "By all the graybeards in the Orient!" he exclaimed, and suddenly stopped pacing the deck. "Tomorrow I'll be seventy, not a day less or a day more, and I still feel spry as a lad."

With hands behind his back and head bent Captain Jans paced toward the stern. And when he chanced to glance at the anchor, attached to the end of a long cable, a wonderful idea flashed to mind.

"Ha, ha! Let the Horned One come for my soul!" Captain Jans cried, roaring with laughter. His ruddy face crinkled, his eyes were like stars. That night Captain Jans was too pleased to sleep. Instead, he sat in his chair with mug and pipe and planned for the future. "I'll circle the globe another seven times, and stop in Friesland once more. Then I'll head toward the islands for spices and silks, and chests of pearls." After a lifetime, Jans still had not sailed enough. In the next world he hoped there'd be need of a captain, to guide boats through uncharted seas!

As he started his rounds, next day, the Captain's eyes were bright, his step brisk. When fierce winds bellied the sails and tipped the tall masts, he smiled in his beard. "Prepare for emergency," Captain Jans shouted to the sailors, and examined the anchor again.

"Good morning, Captain. How wisely you speak," jeered the Devil, who'd hopped up behind. "Today you'll celebrate your birthday in Hell. I'm carrying you on my back, in case you have any notions of—"

"Ho, ho, is that so?" the Captain shouted, swinging around to meet the Devil's mean eyes. "I'd not be in such a hurry, if I were you. Before we start, I have a task for you."

The Devil quaked with fear in spite of himself. After Pieter's swindling, all he got was a thrashing when he arrived in Hell, empty-handed. And when his deal with Ebbel fell through— The Devil winced at thought of the humiliation he suffered then. If he failed a third time, he'd sizzle in his own fires. "If you have a task, name it, old man," he said boldly, and added, "and with these rough seas, don't count on escaping."

"I'd not for a minute," Captain Jans assured him, eyes glinting in a way the Devil didn't like one bit. "And don't be uneasy. The task I'm giving you is so simple even you can do it, I'm sure. You're to take this anchor and walk behind the ship, making sure to keep the chain taut. When I shout 'Avast,' all you have to do is drop anchor."

"Bah, if that's all," the Devil snorted, more relieved than he

cared to admit. "Even a young Devil, with eyes shut, could do *that!*" At an early age, Devils were taught to walk on water, easily as on dry land. Plainly, Jans wasn't so clever as his brothers. It wouldn't be long before he'd be on the way to Hell with this prize, the Devil reflected jubilantly.

With a shriek of joy, the Devil snatched the anchor and sprang over the stern of the ship. Then, holding the anchor in both hands, he ran nimbly over the waves. With an insolent grin on his ugly face, he shouted, "Shake a leg, Captain Jans, or do I wait all day for your command?"

"You'll not wait long," muttered Captain Jans, running toward the bow. The wind was blowing a gale now, the ship leaping. "Let go, all!" he yelled. A knowing smile flitted over his face as the wind-filled sails speeded the ship.

The vessel bounded forward, with the Devil running behind. He was so sure of his victim now that when Captain Jans barked, "Drop anchor. Hold!" he did so, not thinking of consequences. As the anchor plummeted down, down, the ship stopped with a jerk, *but the Devil did not.* He was still loping along merrily—smack into the stern! The next thing the Devil knew, he was flying high above the topmost mast, and screaming with terror, livid with fright, he landed with a thunderous splash in the waves before the bow.

"Lively, lads, lively. Up anchor!" bawled Captain Jans. The next instant, the ship sprang ahead. Just as the sputtering Devil bobbed up to the surface, the vessel plowed over his black body.

"It mashed him thin as a Frisian pancake," chuckle the old men of Haulerwyk, who still tell the tale.

"But it didn't *kill* him," many claim. After a while the Devil, his body broken and bruised, and his tail dragging, reached Hell without Captain Jans. "After his horrible lesson, the Devil's let our mariners alone," they add proudly. "Never again did he have dealings with them!"

As to the fate of the three clever brothers, the old ones agree. "They lived so long no one remembers when they died," they say. "For hundreds of years, we Frisians have enjoyed the fruit of their labor. Thanks to Pieter, our *roggebrood* [rye bread] is the tastiest in the world. Because of Ebbel, our sawmills are the busiest, our woods the best. And when it comes to sailing ships that skim like birds across our lakes, whom do we thank save Captain Jans?"

10 THE SIGN AT THE SMITHY DOOR
(Russia)

Once upon a time, long, long ago, the poor blacksmith Dimitri plied his trade in a village in Old Mother Russia. Yet—though he worked hard—he was miserably poor, as were all the villagers around him. They could barely pay him in barter for shoeing their skinny nags, and then it was in potatoes and meal. Only the rich *Boyár*, the noble lord, who lived in the manor house on the hill with his withered old wife, paid with money. And then poor Dimitri had one kopek to rub against another in his pocket. But never for long! There was always something to buy for his family.

One day, the old man was so hungry at his work that no matter how much he tightened his belt, his stomach still growled. He threw down his tools and stared at the onion-shaped steeple of the village church. "I've done all I can," he shouted. "Now let's see what the saints can do for me," and he stomped off to the church.

But on his knees in the empty church, Dimitri couldn't pray. His thoughts wandered, and also his eyes, until they rested on the grinning Devil in the picture of Judgment Day. "I say, you're a well-fed Devil!" the blacksmith exclaimed, at last, for he couldn't help but admire the sleek look of the creature, and the jaunty set of his horns, and the twirl of the long forked tail.

The longer the blacksmith stared at the dark ugly face, the harder he found it to remember his prayers. And after a while, he forgot to ask the saints to help him, for he'd had an idea that couldn't fail.

Dimitri rose stiffly and lighted a candle. Then he placed it before the Devil in the Judgment Day picture. "You're a smart fellow," the old man said. "I daresay, there isn't a craft or a trade you don't know. Supposing I were to make you a patron of mine, showed you honor and respect. Would you help me then, make me prosperous, rich, for seven years, say, if—" The blacksmith paused, uneasy in spite of himself. "If I agreed to the usual terms?"

Now what the Devil replied, we don't know. But when Dimitri ran from the church, he was smiling. He'd made a good bargain. And back at the smithy, he put up a sign. On it was a Devil, complete with horns, cloven hooves and a handsome tail. "There, friend," the blacksmith said, hanging the symbol above the door. "You're as fine a fellow as the Devil of the Judgment Day!"

When Dimitri's son, Ivan, a simple pious youth who'd learned the blacksmith's trade as well as his father, pointed out that the sign was ungodly, the old man clucked, "Tut, tut. It's only a sign. Wait and see," he added, slapping the lad's shoulder. "People from far and near will hear of it. Now we'll have plenty of business."

And Dimitri was right. Soon fame of his work spread to other villages. Even Boyárs from distant towns sent mares for shoeing at the smithy with the sign—and bid their servants pay in gold.

Week after week, trade was good. And when no one was about, Dimitri greeted the image of the Devil at the door with a cheery "Good day, partner," or a "Hail, fellow citizen." And on leaving the smithy, the blacksmith doffed his cap and bid the Evil One a pleasant "Good Night."

Now the blacksmith had meat on his table, just like the rich Boyár on the hill. Dimitri's wife rustled to church in a silk apron. The children had sandals for their feet, Ivan a sheepskin hat for his head.

Yet, as Dimitri waxed richer, he feared Ivan might guess the true state of affairs. His troubled looks lately, when he regarded the sign prompted his father to say, one day, "With things going so well now, Son, I don't need you at the smithy. With more than a dozen pairs of hands can do, I can afford to be choosy. Your mother and I have decided that, before settling down here, you should travel, see the world as a rich man's son."

Ivan, a homebody at heart, protested he didn't want to leave his father alone with the smithy. "Ho, don't let *that* worry you," said the old man with a wink. "Now I'm so prosperous, I could have a partner should I want one."

Ivan set out, at last, to see the world. And what with his family so well provided for, Dimitri was well pleased with his bargain with the Devil. But after the first year ended and then the second, and the third had started, the blacksmith began to have qualms. He hated to think of leaving the fine life he was enjoying, thanks to his patron. "Since I'm so good to the Devil, respectful and all, maybe he'll not claim me at the end of seven years," Dimitri reasoned. After that, he took special pains to make conciliatory remarks each time he passed the sign. All the same, he couldn't help worrying.

As the sixth year drew to a close, and then the seventh, Dimitri worried more than ever. After supper, he took to sitting for hours, staring at the wall. And if a board squeaked or a mouse scurried, he blanched to the roots of his hair.

Then one night, Dimitri was so discouraged he lay down like a stone on the warm ledge where the old folks sleep, next to the tiled stove. "Come morning, I'll rise like a loaf of bread," he said.

But Dimitri didn't rise, for in the night the Devil crept up and claimed what was his. "A bargain's a bargain, old man. Time's up," he gloated and heaved the blacksmith's soul to his back. "You've had your fun, now it's my turn!"

And so the old man died and was buried. His son, Ivan, hastened home from his travels and took over the smithy. But when he did so, he showed no respect for the sign of the Devil. The only reason he left it where it was, was because now the place was known far and wide by it.

"Take that!" Ivan growled each day, at the door of the smithy, and rapped the sign smartly with his hammer. "And if you dare poke your nose inside, you get worse," he added, and spat in scorn at the grinning face.

Now if there's one thing the Devil can't endure, it's contempt, so he vowed revenge. "I'll make the stupid fool pay for this," he muttered. "I'll teach him to spit at my image."

First, the fiend set about making Ivan poor as his father was once. But even when the youth had to move to a humble cottage, and live on soup and potatoes, he stayed cheerful.

Ivan soon discovered that whether he worked harder and ate less, or whether he didn't, mattered little. Everything at the smithy was at sixes and sevens. The fire wouldn't burn, the bellows wouldn't blow, and as to customers, they faded away.

One day, when the Devil saw that regardless of what misfortunes he sent, Ivan plodded along with patience, he changed himself into a swarthy youth. Then he presented himself at the smithy door. "Good morning, Master," he said. "Could you use an apprentice?"

"By the beard of Little Saint Peter, that I could," grunted Ivan, not glancing up from the dead fire. "But with business so bad, I'll not need help."

"Nevertheless, I hear you're a master blacksmith, and I want to learn the trade well—then be my own man," the youth said—too glibly, Ivan thought. "No one can build a fire, heat coals, or blow bellows better than I."

Ivan looked the fellow over. The young man seemed strong and willing. Still, at first sight, the blacksmith didn't fancy those dark glowing eyes. There was something about them that made him uneasy. But before he had a chance to turn him down, the lad had taken the poker out of his hands. "Let me try," he said and stood before the forge. "Two pairs of hands are better than one, and with me to help, things are sure to pick up."

Before Ivan knew it, the fire was roaring. The stranger had a knack, he reluctantly admitted and agreed to teach him the trade on the finest of terms. "What's your name, boy?" he asked kindly. "Where do you come from?"

"People call me Misha," the youth answered. "And I come from over yonder." He waved a hand vaguely and bent over the forge.

In spite of the Master's misgivings, Misha quickly proved he was a born blacksmith. No helper ever heated a forge faster, or shaped a shoe with greater skill. "Soon everything I do, you'll do better," Ivan told him.

In time, the blacksmith grew more trustful of his helper. "I misjudged him," Ivan told his wife. "The lad's apt, and eager to learn. Whether I'm there or not, he does his work well."

One day, on entering the smithy after his usual scornful salute to the sign at the door, Ivan found Misha hard at work. "There's a fair, Master, in the next village," he said, glancing up from the anvil with those strange glowing eyes. "If you've a mind to take the Mistress, I'll look after things here."

Ivan hesitated. Business had been looking up lately. And what with the lad eager to prove himself, and the blacksmith's wife wanting trinkets he'd had to deny so long, he decided to accept his helper's offer.

"You'll be surprised, when you return, at all I have done," Misha said and pounded lustily. But no sooner had the Master left than the blows grew vicious. "One for every time you've hammered my image at the door," he muttered, sending sparks in all directions. "One for each spit at the face. And now for my vengeance! I'll teach that pasty-faced blacksmith a lesson," and he stared hard up the hill at the Boyár's manor.

It wasn't long before hooves clattered over the cobblestones. Misha rushed to the door, hammer in hand. And when the Boyár's barouche rounded the corner, he shouted at the withered old Boyárina, sitting bolt upright inside. "There's new work at the smithy today. We're forging old folks into new."

"Hey, what's that you say?" shrilled the old lady, who cupped her ear with her hand and ordered the coachman to rein in the horses. She beckoned to the apprentice. "Did I understand rightly, young man?" she demanded, so excited her head bobbed

and her bonnet strings jumped. "Can you forge me into a beautiful young girl? Well, speak up. Can you? Is that true?"

"It's true—for a price," Misha said. "Else would I be shouting at you?"

The old woman, who'd never ceased to mourn her lost youth, groped toward her purse. "If you really mean you *can* do what you say," she rasped, in a trembling voice, "name your price."

"Seven hundred rubles—not one more, or one less," the young smith replied, his eyes glittering.

"Robber!" shrieked the old one, shaking her fist. "Seven hundred rubles! Whoever heard of such a price?"

"Or such a task!" said the Devil, sweeping his eyes over the Boyárina's withered form. Then he shrugged and turned as if to enter the smithy.

"Wait, come back," the old lady implored. "I didn't say I wouldn't pay—only that the sum was great."

When the Boyárina had finally counted one hundred—five hundred—seven hundred rubles into the Devil's outstretched hand, his eyes glowed maliciously.

"Send your coachman to the village for three buckets of milk," Misha ordered and pocketed the rubles. Then he led the Boyárina inside. "First I forge you in fire, then wash you in milk," he remarked.

"And then?" faltered the aged woman uneasily.

"Then you'll step from your bath young as spring, lovely as dawn," the Devil promised, and poked up the fire.

When the coachman returned with the milk, Misha poured it into a tub. "Go now," he said, dismissing the man. "Return for your Mistress in an hour."

And then, when everything was in readiness and the forge blazing hot, Misha caught the Boyárina round the waist in his long blacksmith's tongs. "Ha," he yelled, and pitched her into the roaring furnace. As the flames shot up and the fuel crackled, he watched and rubbed his hands in glee.

When nothing was left of the old lady but bones, Misha gathered them up and threw them sizzling into the milk. "Just wait, Master Ivan," he gloated, stirring them around. "How truly you spoke when you said everything you did, I'd do better!"

When the coachman rolled up to the door, later, a dazzling young girl leaped from the tub. Her eyes were like stars, her lips red as cherries. And the thick plaits around her head shimmered like gold. "I'm young—young!" she exulted, turning her pretty head this way and that, admiring her pretty hands.

And then, without so much as a "thank you" or even a nod, the beautiful creature ran from the door. The coachman's mouth hung open at sight of his Mistress. "Drive me to the Master," she said haughtily and seated herself in the carriage. "I can't wait to see his face when his wife returns, all lovely and young!"

But the Boyár, alas, didn't recognize his old withered wife in the beautiful girl who sprang from the coach—not until she screamed, "What's the matter, you doddering old fool? Are you blind as a bat? Can't you see I'm your wife, all spritely and young, and that I don't want an old husband now?"

"I see too plainly," said the Boyár sadly, for he had adored his withered old woman. "Who made you young? What has happened to you? Even though you're young, there's nothing I can do."

"Oh, yes, there is, and you'll do it unless you want me to leave you," the girl shrilled with a giddy twirl on her toes. "Go to the smithy, order the apprentice to make you into a comely youth again. Then we'll dance all night," she rattled on. "People will gaze at us in envy. 'Who is that beautiful girl and that handsome young man?' they will ask!"

When at last the Boyár learned what had occurred, he refused any part in the strange goings-on. But after his wife had stamped and wept, and then pushed him into the barouche, he reluctantly ordered the coachman to drive him to the smithy.

Ivan, meanwhile, who'd returned from the fair, went to the smithy to see how things were going. He stopped, as usual, at the door and gave the devil face a good whack. Inside, however, he saw no one about. The forge was cold and Misha's tools lay in a careless heap on the floor on top of his leather apron. Strangest of all, there stood the tub that usually held water, half-filled with milk, and milk was splattered all about.

What could it mean, Ivan wondered, scratching his head. After he'd searched everywhere and called his helper by name, and even asked passersby if they'd seen him, the blacksmith concluded, "The boy's learned his trade well. Now he's gone into the world." Still, that didn't account for the milk!

It was then the blacksmith thought he heard mocking laughter. Yet he saw no one, and after he'd poked in dusty corners and called again, he built a fire and set to work. Misha's disappearance had upset him more than he cared to admit, for he'd been good and kind to the strange lad. Soon Ivan was banging the anvil as if his life depended on the noise it took to pound out the rim of a wheel.

Indeed, he was making such a racket he didn't hear the carriage roll up. And when he chanced to glance about and saw the Boyár, Ivan jumped. "Please, make me into a handsome young man at once," the old lord implored, before the blacksmith could bow to him respectfully.

"But I'm a blacksmith, not a magician!" Ivan cried, thinking the old man mad.

"You're a scoundrel—a rascal—that's what you are!" shouted the Boyár. "You turned my old woman into a beautiful girl. Why can't you do as well by me? If you don't, she'll—she'll—" The old voice trailed off wretchedly.

"I've had nothing to do with your wife—let alone make her young," Ivan muttered, more convinced than before that the Boyár had taken leave of his senses.

"Well, if you didn't, your helper did," stormed the old man. Suddenly spying the milk, he shouted. "There—that proves it! My wife said your boy forged her in the furnace, then bathed her in milk. You, the Master, surely can manage the business as well. Of course, if it's money you're after—" he continued, rummaging for his purse. "Here's double what your apprentice demanded." Before Ivan knew it, the Boyár pressed the purse in his hands.

"I don't want money or anything for what I can't do. Only the Devil could do what you ask," Ivan protested as he tried to thrust the money back. The old man wouldn't listen to reason. If the blacksmith refused to do him this service, he, the Boyár, would have him flogged in public, then run from the village. He'd do well to think twice before defying his betters!

By now, Ivan was in a state of terrible confusion, especially since the Devil, who lurked in the shadows, made the Boyár utter even wilder threats. And when he went to the forge and frantically started picking up tools, the blacksmith reluctantly stoked the furnace. Then he sent the coachman home. Scarcely knowing what he was doing, Ivan nipped up his lordship by a leg and threw him into the red-hot forge.

What happened next is too horrible to tell. When Ivan finally raked out the Boyár's charred bones and cast them into the milk, nothing happened. No handsome young man leaped from the bath, even after one—and then two—and finally, three hours had dragged by. The blacksmith peered anxiously into the tub. He poked at the bones. At last, overcome by the awful truth, he cried wildly, "I've killed the old man! The Boyár is dead, and I've murdered him!"

Just at that moment the beautiful young Boyárina burst into

the smithy, demanding to know where her husband was. "He's not home yet," she cried, sweeping her eyes about the smithy. When she caught sight of the charred bones floating in the milk and Ivan staring at the tub, she ran out, shrieking, "You've killed my husband! You've murdered the Boyár!"

"And so you have, Master," taunted a voice from somewhere behind. "She'll send for the Starósta [Mayor] and he'll send for the hangman. The villagers will be here soon, to drag you to the gallows and hang you as a murderer, unless—"

"Unless what?" Ivan shouted, and spun around. There in the shadows stood Misha. In the dim light he was more swarthy. Horns rose from his head and he had cloven hooves, and a tail, long and forked on the end. "You, my helper, are the Devil himself. You made me do this!" the blacksmith gasped and drew back in horror.

"Well, Master, I didn't think you'd ever guess," sneered the Devil, his eyes glowing like embers. "But take heart. If you do as I say, I'll save you. I'll revive the Boyár and turn him into a youth. Otherwise," he added, advancing a step, "you'll swing by your neck from a tree."

Already Ivan could hear the howls of the mob. He wavered an instant, but then a desperate plan began to take shape in his mind. "What do you want me to do?" he asked and reached toward the hammer on the floor.

"Show me honor, respect. Stop knocking my head and spitting into my face, and I'll make you rich, as I did your father," replied the Devil, so much in earnest he didn't notice Ivan's fingers close over the hammer handle. "All I ask is your soul."

"And all you'll get is this," roared Ivan, lunging at the Devil. With the hammer high in his hands, the blacksmith thwacked it onto the Devil's head—once—twice—THREE times. "I'll show you honor, respect," he bellowed, and hit again with all the strength of his brawny arms.

At first the Devil howled with pain, then sank to his knees and whined for mercy. But, at last, he lay on the floor, limp and still as an ugly black rag. Ivan reached for his nippers. He pinched up the horrid thing by the long stringy tail. With all his might, he hurled what remained of the Devil into the forge and spat into the flames.

The villagers were closer now, shrieking for his blood. But Ivan hadn't finished his work. He strode to the door, and with one blow shattered the sign into a thousand pieces. "And good riddance to you!" he shouted. Then he scooped them up and tossed them into the furnace, where the flames devoured them with a roar.

Ivan turned slowly. The mob could hang him now. He'd done what he could to undo his grievous crime.

But as Ivan turned to the door, he saw the old Boyár, alive and all in one piece, wrinkled as ever, but smiling. "You have taught me a lesson I'll not forget," the old man said, taking Ivan's calloused hands in his own. "The money I forced on you I want you to keep as a token of my esteem. Few men would have done what you did—and I among them."

Moments later, when the screaming crowd burst into the smithy and saw the Boyár safe and sound, they fell back in wonder. "Fetch my barouche," he ordered. "Then go home. The blacksmith has done no wrong."

Now with the Devil on earth destroyed, and the Boyár alive, and the evil sign burned to ash, Ivan hastened to the church to burn a candle before the saints. "May lust for money, or fear of punishment, never lead me into temptation," he prayed.

Ivan's prayer was answered. To the day of his death he remained pious and good, and the smithy prospered. Though never rich, he and his wife were content—and had more than enough for their needs.

And as for the Boyár, when he reached home and found his wife withered and old again and sobbing her heart out because she had thought him dead, he took her in his arms and comforted her. "Thanks to Our Little Father in Heaven, and the blacksmith, you are yourself and I'm alive," he said.

Some say the aged couple lived to the age of a hundred and three, and that if ever the Boyárina mourned her lost youth, her husband patted her wrinkled hand and said, "To me, you are more beautiful, dear love, than that young shrew who screamed at me. A warm heart in a withered breast is a thousand times better than the cold cruel heart of a beautiful girl."

11

THE DEVILS' GRANNY

(Germany)

The brothers, Fritz and Hans, lived in a village at the edge of the forest. No one ventured there. Just peering down the winding path, overgrown by briers and brush, made people blanch. The trees loomed forbidding and tall, and howls and shrieks came from the woods at night. During the day there were strange chop-choppings— as though three hundred and three woodcutters were felling trees. "In there Devils live! They're chopping wood for the fires of Hell," the villagers muttered. "That path leads straight into Hell."

That's what young Hans had heard, ever since his grandfather dangled him on his knee, as a lad. Every day, on his way to work for his older brother, Fritz, who was married now and rich, and lived in the big house on the hill, Hans pelted past the woods fast as his long legs would take him. It wasn't that he was afraid—just that the place had a scary look.

Fritz was a butcher. When their parents died, he had raised young Hans. And the lad, who liked to cook and experiment and had a natural gift for putting together a pinch of this and a dab of that, had kept house for Fritz and served up tasty meals.

Now that Hans was old enough to become an apprentice and handier than most, Fritz was teaching him the trade. Already, the youth made the best liver sausages of anyone for miles about. "When I scrape enough together, I'll have my own sausage shop," he told his brother.

"Well, I'd not count on it for a while," grunted Fritz, who was miserly as well as jealous of his younger brother's skill. "You're such a blockhead at learning, you can't expect me to pay wages, not for three years at least, especially with all you owe for the years I took care of you," he added meanly.

Yet, in spite of his scoffing, Fritz depended on the youth more than he cared to admit, especially when it came time for sausage making. Even he conceded the lad had a knack for concocting sausage meat. And though Fritz watched him like a lynx, he'd never tell him how much of this or that went into his trough. "That's *my* secret!" he'd tease and watch his brother's fat face turn red.

Just the same, Fritz got even. For aside from tossing Hans a few coppers and a scraggle of bacon or stew and a whole liver sausage when they made them, he didn't care because the lad was poor. Now that the butcher no longer needed him—what with a wife to cook and keep house—he let Hans live alone in the shabby cottage their grandfather had left them. "Once a fool, always a fool," muttered Fritz, who'd grown rich on dishonesty. "Whether I help him, or whether I don't, makes no difference. He'd give his shirt to the first beggar who asks."

And this was true, for Hans was generous, as Fritz was mean. To share the little he had was the youth's joy. If he met a needy woman, he'd say, "Good Mother, drop this bone into your kettle," though it meant he'd have no soup. If a beggar knocked at the door he'd make a packet of his meager meal. "Take these bits. I'm not hungry," he'd tell the poor one.

Yet with a trade to learn, Hans didn't complain. What Fritz chose to give, he accepted with thanks, and eked out a living with odd jobs. But one day, when his brother snarled he was late when he came to work early— "We're making sausages today, as you well know, yet you dawdle like a snail—" he stood up for himself. "To teach you a lesson, I've a mind not to give you the liver sausage you always expect," the butcher blustered.

Hans, tying on his apron, laughed good-naturedly. "For that, I'll take two, Brother," said he. "For if you listen, you'll hear the chimes in the church tower striking seven now."

Fritz's fat face turned purple. "Two liver sausages! Whoever heard of such impudence," he muttered. "One might suppose sausages grew on trees."

Hans said no more. He set to work with a will. He ground the meat and cooked the liver. As tantalizing odors filled the kitchen, Fritz sniffed and drooled. He watched his brother's hands move swiftly from mixing spoon to spices, from spices to salt, a dash of this, a pinch of that, then stirrings and beatings that deafened the ear. Yet for all the butcher's watching, the hands flew faster than eye could follow. When it came time to force the stuffing into cases, he was none the wiser as to how it was made.

At last, dozens of sausages—tiny links and great fat ones, two feet long—hung from the rafters, like dozens of brown shining beads. Hans scraped his trough and scrubbed his pans, then hung his apron on the peg near the door. "Well, Brother?" he said, a maddening grin on his face.

"Now your work's done, I suppose you're expecting your sausage," snarled Fritz, and selected the smallest he could find.

"Thank you, Brother," Hans said. "Now a second one, please."

Fritz snorted, "A second one, indeed!" Just the same, seeing that Hans wasn't leaving, he threw him another. "To the Devils in Hell with you and your sausages!" screamed the butcher. His brother's good nature—coupled with his laugh and bows—infuriated him further.

Hans started for home, hugging his sausages inside his shirt. "Tonight I'll invite a friend for supper," he planned gleefully. Just then, he reached the woods. For some reason, they looked less dark, less forbidding than usual. The overgrown path was less eerie.

Hans intended to race by. But all at once, an idea popped to mind—an idea that stopped him short in his tracks. He scratched his head. "Well, why not?" he said, his eyes sparkling. "Fritz said, 'To the Devils in Hell with you and your sausages!' "

The more Hans thought about it, the more tempted he was to try his idea, especially since his grandfather used to say, "Remember, lad, though you meet the Devils in Hell, you've nothing to fear, not if you're kind and polite."

Hans had never known Grandfather to be wrong. Besides, if he, Hans, made the long journey to Hell and shared his prize with a Devil, what a fine adventure that would be. It wasn't as though he'd be offering an ordinary sausage. His were the best in the world. "A right tasty bit for any Devil," Hans decided. With a light heart, he plunged down the path and into the woods, where no villager had ever ventured.

But what started as a lark soon proved to be terrifying. For the deeper Hans penetrated the woods the scratchier the brambles, the more dead branches slapped at his face, tore at his hair. To make matters even worse, darkness fell quickly. At last, Hans didn't know whether he was going backward or forward, and when he nearly broke his neck falling over a stone, he muttered, "I'm lost," and decided to sit there the night.

Toward midnight Hans heard shrieks and groans coming from inside the forest. He dozed fitfully, but at dawn the sound of furious choppings brought him to his feet with a start. He stumbled on blindly the rest of the day. He thought he'd die of hunger. Tempted though he was to nibble into the sausages, he decided since he'd come this far without eating, he could hold out for a while.

When darkness again fell, Hans stretched on a flat rock, too exhausted to move or even mind the thirst that now consumed him. Clasping his sausages tightly, he murmured, "I never d-dreamed it was such a long way to H-Hell—" and fell asleep instantly.

When Hans woke, next day, he was so stiff he thought he was dead. But when he found he could get up and then walk, things looked brighter. He plodded on doggedly. When at last he reached a clearing with a small house, he wanted to shout. He hurried to the door, but before he could knock, it swung open. There stood such a frightening old she-Devil, in a red-and-white checkered apron, and a ruffled cap through which two horns protruded. Hans thought his knees would give way. "G-good day, G-Granny Devil. I hope you are well," he stammered politely, remembering Grandfather.

"Well, young man," rasped the Devil. The eyes behind her spectacles glittered. Her forked tail switched. "What I'd like to know is what brings you here, and how you happened to make the journey alone."

Hans dove inside his shirt and pulled out his sausages. The feel of them in his hands gave him courage. "It's these," he said, swallowing hard. "The liver sausages I made for my butcher brother, Fritz. When he gave them to me, after I'd helped him, he sent me to Hell. But this is as far as I've got. One's for you, one for me— and they're best roasted," he added.

"I'd like to meet that butcher brother of yours!" muttered Granny Devil, as if to herself. Then her leathery face creased into a smile. "Liver sausages, eh? It's been ever so long since I've tasted any," she said, sniffing. "Come in, lad. It's easy to see the journey's tuckered you out. I'll stir up the fire and roast the sausages while you rest and tell me about yourself." So saying, the old Devil dusted a stool with her apron. As she bustled around, Hans' eyes swept over the kitchen, the shining copper pots, and the bed with a ruffled curtain at the bottom, in the corner.

Granny roasted the sausages. Then she set the table and took a loaf from the oven, poured out wine. When she bid Hans sit opposite her, he felt quite easy, and chatted and talked, as with an old friend. "One day I'll be my own man, have my own sausage shop," he confided to Granny. "Of course, that's years and years ahead, what with no money and making my own way," he added with a sigh.

From over her spectacles Granny's eyes glowed brightly. "Tut, tut, lad, if this sausage is a sample of your work, it could be sooner," she said with a loud smack. Then she sat licking her fingers and stared at Hans thoughtfully.

Hans flushed with pride. "I'm glad you like my liver sausage, Granny. I thought you would," he said and added, " 'Twas your loaf, and the wine, as made them a feast."

The afternoon wore on pleasantly. Granny sat in her rocker before the fire and told Hans about her seven grandsons. "They live with me," she said. "A wilder lot of demons you never saw!"

Hans was uneasy, in spite of himself. "W-where are they?" he faltered.

"In the forest, chopping wood for bonfires," said Granny, with a wink. "They leave at dawn and return at dusk, hungry as horses." She rose and peered from the window, then stirred the contents of the big black pot on the hearth. "They'll be here soon and if supper isn't ready, things will go badly for you."

Hans gasped, more frightened than before.

"Don't be afraid," grunted Granny Devil. "Just do as I say. Hide under my bed and don't make a sound. Don't come out till I call you. Quick now! I hear them coming!"

So did Hans. He scuttled for the corner and crawled behind the bed curtain in the nick of time. The next instant, the door shot open. Seven frightening young Devils burst into the kitchen, with howls and shrieks that turned the blood in his veins to ice. Still he was curious, and if he lived through this, he wanted to remember everything.

By lying on his stomach and peering under the curtains, Hans found he could see everything, and still not be seen. The demons were husky fellows, with big muscles and whiplike forked tails. Their horns were stubby and short, their jaws hungry and wide. Most terrifying of all were the teeth—sharp and cruel as wolf fangs— and the pointed ears that bristled with long coarse hairs.

"I smell the flesh of a human. Who's been here?" roared the Seventh Devil, rolling his round marble eyes.

"No one, you fool," Granny Devil rasped, slapping plates on the table with a bang that made Hans jump. "Fetch those bowls. Help me ladle soup."

"We're hungry as horses!" shouted the First Devil, licking his lips.

"Then sit down and eat," Granny Devil ordered. "When the soup's gone, there's stew. I'd advise you to be quick if each wants his share."

Fearsome grunts followed, scrapings on bowls. And when the demons finished off their soup and stew and the last crumb of bread, they stretched on the floor before the hearth. After their loud snores shook the rafters, Granny Devil climbed into bed. Then Hans closed his eyes.

In spite of his terror, Hans slept so soundly he didn't even

hear the Devils when they roared away at dawn. He couldn't remember where he was, when Granny Devil called, "Wake up, lad.
It's safe to come out. They've gone to the forest."

"Good morning, Granny Devil. I hope you rested well," said
Hans, crawling from under the curtains.

"Better than you, I daresay," the old she-Devil chuckled,
dishing out porridge. After breakfast, she pointed out a shortcut to
the village. "And here's a present for you," she said kindly, "since
you were thoughtful enough to bring me a sausage."

"But I don't want a present, not for sharing a sausage," protested Hans.

"Never mind. Hold out your hand," Granny Devil commanded
and placed a coarse gray hair on his palm. "It's from my head and
it's magic." She cackled delightedly. "Only mind what I say. Close
your hand now. Don't look again till you reach home."

Hans thanked the Devils' Granny and bid her farewell. All
the way home he wondered about the hair. When he finally got there
and opened his hand, he stared in amazement. For lo! the hair had
vanished. In its place he was grasping a small bag—a bag lumpy and
round, with seven gold pieces inside. "Gold!" exclaimed Hans, his
jaw dropping. "Granny Devil hinted I might have my own shop
sooner than I thought!"

When Hans went to his brother's, next day, he ranted and
roared that giving him two sausages had turned his head so he hadn't
shown up for work—three days running! When he paid no attention
and told Fritz he was going to open a small place of his own, the
butcher sneered meanly, "So, my young brother's going into business,
eh? On what, may I ask? Not anything he'll get from me!"

"I hadn't counted on that, Brother," replied Hans and kept
his own counsel.

But as weeks and months passed and Hans had a modest shop
and prospered in everything, Fritz bit his nails in envy and rage.
Thought of the young upstart's success tortured the butcher night
and day. Besides, everyone for miles around was flocking to Hans'
shop, clamoring for his sausages, blabbering about his kindness to
the poor.

At last, unable to contain his jealousy longer, Fritz demanded,
one day, "Where did you get money for all this?" His greedy eyes
swept the shiny brown links, the fat coils of sausages that hung from
rafters, burst from shelves.

"From the Devils in Hell, dear Brother, where you sent me

and my liver sausages," laughed Hans. "They gave me the gold."

"Gold—for two measly sausages!" the butcher shouted hoarsely. Then he shook his fist at Hans, and rushed from the door. Two could play the same game!

Fritz lost no time in making a sausage. For days and weeks he sweated and toiled to make one so huge he could scarcely clasp it in his pudgy arms. Of course, the stuffing wasn't like his brother's. The sly fellow had taken care to see that he, Fritz, who'd raised him and trained him for years, shouldn't learn the secret of that. Still, Devils wouldn't know the difference, he reasoned. With them, what counted was size. If they'd give so much gold for one small bite, what wouldn't they offer for a liver sausage big enough to feed a multitude?

When he'd finished his sausage, Fritz lugged it to Hell, though how he managed or how long the journey took, no one remembers, after so many years. But when he finally reached the clearing, he was huffing and puffing. His eyes were glassy, his temper short.

And when the Devils' Granny opened her door and peered over her spectacles at the red-faced butcher, he snapped, "Well, what are you staring at, you leather-faced old Devil?"

The round eyes behind the spectacles flared wickedly. "At that fine sausage," grated Granny, tapping her forked tail on the floor. "I was expecting it."

"Oh, you were, were you?" taunted Fritz. "At your age you probably haven't enough teeth to bite into it! I made this for the Devils who gave my brother gold for a sausage too small to see! Where are they, anyway?" he asked, glancing about.

"In the forest chopping wood—if they're the ones you want to see," said Granny, an evil smile twisting her lips. "You'll hear them soon, when they return for supper. Come in. Sit down at the table—if you care to wait, that is."

Fritz didn't need to be urged. He dragged in his sausage and heaved it to the table. Then he eased himself to a stool. But it wasn't long before bloodcurdling shrieks made him blanch with terror.

"Granny, Granny, we smell human flesh," the Devils screeched. "We're hungry as horses. Where's our supper?"

"It's there—*waiting!*" thundered Granny Devil in a terrible voice and pointed to Fritz.

The wretched butcher tried to scream, but no sound came from his throat. With wild howls the Devils swooped upon their prey.

They tore him to bits and gobbled his flesh. Then they fell upon the huge sausage. Before the moon rose, they had finished that. Too full to move, the seven Devils dropped to the floor.

Long after the Devils' snores racked the rafters, Granny sat in her chair. "It goes hard with the greedy once they reach Hell," she muttered, her eyes glittering. "Especially if someone who's generous and kind gets here first. Then we Devils can afford a choice!"

When Granny Devil rose, at last, and climbed into bed, her eyes were glowing like the embers on the hearth.

12

SAINT SAVA
AND THE DEVIL
(Serbia)

One day when God saw a Devil creep out of Hell and begin to prowl among the farms and villages of the Serbian countryside, He sent for the great Saint Sava. "Disguise yourself. Visit earth," commanded God. "Thwart the Evil One in his search for souls. Send him back to Hell, too frightened to show his face on earth again."

The following day, accordingly, Saint Sava in the guise of a village priest with shaven head and coarse brown robe trudged a narrow path winding up a mountain. On one side was a cliff, on the other a chasm. And in the valley below lay fields of barley and rye, and a village with thatched houses and an onion-domed church.

The day was fine, the sky blue. Despite his years and plump figure, the disguised Saint swung briskly up the slope—so briskly, in fact, that on turning a sharp bend, a pop-eyed Devil almost ran into him.

The demon was plainly up to no good. He was bounding toward the village on cloven goat feet. His wicked face was eager, his forked tail jaunty. "Ho, Brother! Greetings and God bless you," the priest called out cheerily and stood in the middle of the path.

"A blessing! What's that to me?" rasped the Devil and edged aside to pass the priest. The demon glared, but even so, the stupid fellow didn't budge. Instead, he stood there blocking the way. He smiled and leaned on his stick. And what with his bulk and the lack of space, the Devil couldn't squeeze by.

"How are you, friend?" the priest asked kindly.

"What's that to you?" snarled the Devil and tried to sidle by. He didn't like priests, and the sight of the cross at the old one's waist made him uneasy, in spite of himself.

The priest acted as if he had the rest of the day for idle chitchat. "Where are you going in such a hurry?" he now asked.

"As if that were your business," snapped the Devil and switched his tail.

"It might be if we were partners and made a bargain." The priest chuckled.

So that was the way the wind blew! The Devil's eyes suddenly brightened. To snare a priest's soul meant promotion! Besides, with

111

this old fuddy the task would be easy. But a Devil must be cautious. "What, if anything, is on your mind?" he asked.

"I want to raise my own food, on shares," the Saint said. "As a priest, I'm poor though through the years I've scrimped and saved, a dinar here, a dinar there, from gifts at weddings or wakes. As partners, with a hired field between us, we'd stand to make a tidy profit, in three years, say. Half of everything would be yours, half mine. I'd be willing to do the work," added the priest. "And you could choose what to raise and which part of the crop you want— what's on top, or what's underneath the ground. If you chose right and didn't lose your temper—"

"If I chose right!" the Devil sneered, his eyes glittering. "I always do."

"Then there's nothing to bother you," said the Saint, "unless you get angry."

"And suppose I do?" the Devil leered. "What then?"

"You'd agree to return to Hell forever," said the priest. "But to make things fair, if I lost my temper—"

"I'd lug you there, like a sack of potatoes," the Devil shouted gleefully. "What would you say to that, old man?"

The Saint smiled contentedly. "I'd say, fair enough, Brother," he replied and added, "But remember, you can't afford to lose your temper, not if you want to stay up here!"

And so it was agreed. The two rented a piece of land and the Devil proposed they raise turnips as the first crop. The Saint plowed and sowed and tended the plants. The Devil, who came often to inspect the field, gloated over their sturdiness. He could tell who'd get the better of the deal!

One day, when the turnip tops looked like an ocean of green and Saint Sava was hoeing, his back bent over the long straight rows, up hopped the Devil from behind. "Good day, Partner," he rasped. "I see you're hard at work." He spoke with condescension, though sight of the thriving plants pleased him more than he'd a mind to admit.

"Good morning, Brother," replied the Saint, glancing up. "I thought I'd see you soon."

"Oh, you did, did you?" the Devil jeered. "I suppose you hoped I'd not show up, now it's time to decide on my share of the crop."

"Which part do you choose, Brother—what grows on top of the ground, or what lies underneath?" asked the Saint.

The Devil scratched his head. For all his bluff, he wasn't a

farmer. He knew nothing about turnips or anything that grows from God's earth. But sweeping the green tops with greedy eyes, he chortled, "Need you ask, old man? My share's all that grows on top."

"So shall it be, Brother," said Saint Sava. "And of course, if you've made a mistake, you'll still have two more tries."

The demon's eyes flared meanly. He opened his mouth. But before the angry words came out, he bit his tongue. Turning, he stumped away quickly, muttering about mealymouthed priests.

As the days came and went, the Devil was so busy elsewhere that he didn't come again to inspect the turnip crop. He didn't see the thriving tops gradually wither and sear, and then flop to the ground. He didn't know that underneath, the roots grew round and fat.

At last the time came for the harvest. On that day, when the Saint jogged to the field in an empty cart drawn by a nag, the Devil was waiting and lashing his tail.

"Greetings, Brother, God bless you," Saint Sava called from his cart. "I see you're here for your share of the crop." So saying, he hopped to the ground with his spade.

"My share, indeed!" shrilled the Devil, pointing to the shriveled tops. "What have you done, you—you—?"

"I have tended our crop," the priest said calmly. "This is how turnips grow. See?" He dug into the earth and lifted a fat turnip to show his partner.

The Devil sputtered. His wicked face grew darker. And then before angry words burst from his lips he stamped away. The sounds of turnips rattling into the priest's cart filled him with rage.

In the second year of their partnership, the Devil decided to raise wheat. He'd not let the old one outsmart him again. No indeed! He, the Devil, didn't intend to make the same mistake twice. Even he knew what a showing wheat made on top. Wheat roots might reach clear to China, he decided, remembering the turnips.

The Devil watched anxiously until the seed sprouted and the first green points pricked the earth. When the shoots grew straight and tall, and then the green stalks turned to gold, he rejoiced. But when he saw plump heads of grain appear on each stalk, he kicked his heels in delight. The dry wheat tops couldn't be good for anything, he reasoned. A rich yield of food lay in the roots!

"For my part. I'll take all that's under the ground," the Devil told the Saint, one day. "And don't think you'll swindle me a second time, old man," he added menacingly.

The Saint smiled and said nothing. But on the day appointed for harvesting the grain, he'd already cut the wheat with his scythe and bound the grain into sheaves, before the Devil appeared down the road. At his heels was a band of demons. They were shrieking and dancing. Over their shoulders they swung shovels and picks.

"Ho, Partner," shouted the Devil in high spirits. "I'm late but I had to get helpers. I see you've cut your share of the harvest. Just wait till you see mine!" At a signal the demons swooped upon the field. They dug into the earth with their shovels. They hacked at it with their picks.

"Good luck, Brother," Saint Sava said and tossed the sheaves into the waiting cart. At last, he climbed to the seat and picked up the reins, though he seemed in no hurry to drive off.

Meanwhile the demons, who'd swarmed like black flies among the stubble, started to jeer. When, in spite of furious pickings and scrabblings deep inside the ground, all they unearthed were coarse stringy roots, they shrilled, "Master, where's that crop you hired us to dig?" Then they dangled before the stunned eyes of the Devil the scraggly roots they'd dug up.

At sight of his share of the harvest, the Devil blanched. And no sooner had the demons spread ugly wings and streaked away like black ravens in the sky than he burst into tears. "You—you," he blubbered, turning on Saint Sava. "You've shamed me—tricked me again."

"Nonsense, Brother, and mind your temper," said Saint Sava, a smile twitching at the corners of his mouth. "You got what you bargained for—what's under the ground. You still have another chance." Then he clucked to the nag and rattled off toward the village.

Alone in the field, the Devil hunched on a stone. His shoulders drooped. And as to his tail, that lay on the ground like a limp black rope.

The Devil's eyes swept the stubble drearily. Two years wasted and nothing to show so far! The priest had bilked him twice. He'd do so again, given the chance. And all because he, a hard-working Devil, wasn't a farmer. In a wave of self-pity he thought of the maddening smirk on the old man's face. He'd shown no sign of losing his temper in spite of taunts and threats!

The Devil squirmed uneasily. He knew what to expect if he didn't get the priest's soul in his clutches, the third time around. The Master Devil had made matters clear, last time, when the demon returned to Hell empty-handed.

The Devil sat brooding, wondering what to do next. If only he could devise some way to upset the old scoundrel, think of something he couldn't raise. Dawn was creeping across the meadow before the Devil leaped to his feet. "Goats!" he shouted, prancing about. "Goats are contrary creatures—contrary enough to make even a priest lose his temper!" Since his partner wanted to raise his own food, the demon felt certain he'd agree to raising goats. They provided milk for both drinking and making cheese.

When the Devil slid away in the gray light, his tail was erect. He was chortling. Devils knew about goats!

Some days later, when the Devil proposed they raise goats, instead of another crop, Saint Sava agreed. "As you please, Brother, we'll raise goats. And this time, instead of choosing your share of the crop, you'll choose goats." The only thing is," he added, "if you muddle—"

"If I muddle—ha—" The Devil shouted with laughter. "Whoever heard of a Devil muddling with goats!"

"Nevertheless, if you muddle, you'll return to Hell at once, and never show your face on earth again," said Saint Sava sternly, as if the Devil hadn't interrupted.

When the partners found a herd of brown goats to their liking and Saint Sava said, "Let's drive them up the mountain, and divide them on the way," a cunning look crept into the Devil's face. Things were going better than he'd hoped. On the winding path, with the priest ahead, he'd have a chance to give the creatures sly proddings and kicks. Who could tell what the silly things might do then?

But even the best plans of the Devil can go astray, and when Saint Sava called from somewhere ahead, "Here's a stream, Brother, with no way for goats to reach the other side, except to swim," the Devil quickly decided to let his plan wait awhile.

Saint Sava, meanwhile, had a plan that wouldn't wait. At the bank of the stream, he said, "Let's divide the flock now. Half of the goats belong to you, half to me. When they ford the stream, which do you choose—the goats that hold their tails up when they swim, or those with them down?"

The Devil, caught unaware, rubbed his swarthy chin. He scratched his dark head. What was this nonsense about up or down tails? All he knew was, goats were goats! Of course, if the old one were bluffing, or up to more tricks— "I'll choose the goats that hold their tails *down*," shouted the Devil, for the priest stood there smiling, staring at his face.

No sooner had the words left the Devil's lips than the priest drove the goats through the water. And then, to his horror, the Devil saw every animal from biggest to smallest lift its tail as it floundered through the water.

The eyes of the Devil popped. His face turned ashen gray. He bellowed like a bull. In mortification and rage he lunged at the Saint. "So—you shifty-eyed village priest," the demon roared. "You tried to outsmart the Devil!"

But the Saint stepped aside nimbly. "Tried and did," said he in a voice that made the Evil One shake with terror. "I've outwitted you and you've lost your temper," the holy man went on. "Now out of my sight! Get back to Hell. Never again return to earth."

When the priest had finished, the Serbian people say the Devil skulked away, tail between his legs. "From then until now, the Evil One's not dared show his face in our land," they continue. "But as to Saint Sava, he was our first Archbishop. He is the patron saint of the Serbs."

13 THE GIRL WHO CLUNG TO THE DEVIL'S BACK

(Czechoslovakia)

Andulko was the prettiest girl for miles around, and her clothes were the prettiest, too. For her mother—who hoped to marry her well—worked her aprons with poppies and roses, and sewed yards of lace on her petticoats.

Yet, for all her finery, her sparkling blue eyes and curls that shone like gold in the sun, the girl had no suitors. Andulko, who never was known to say a kind word, was the most disliked girl in the whole village. If a young man invited her to dance, or asked her to go to the fair, she replied in some horrid way. If the lad were clumsy, or had big hands and feet, she'd call him on oaf. If he had red hair, she'd say she didn't like carrot-tops.

Andulko, alas, had a nasty tongue and an even nastier temper. The lads learned to look the other way whenever she appeared. "Handsome is, as handsome does," they'd whisper. And after a while, with no one to ask her out or pay her pretty compliments, the girl found herself moping at home.

Sundays were the dreariest days in the week. After church, other girls met with the boys in the village square. Dressed in their best bodices and caps, they danced away the afternoon. With rosy cheeks and flying ribbons, they twisted and twirled in the arms of young men. At last, breathless and laughing, they gathered to sing and stuff sweets, at the inn on the square.

"I hate Sundays," Andulko told her mother, one especially dismal Sunday. She stamped her foot and turned her back quickly, to hide the tears in her eyes.

Her mother sighed deeply. "With your looks, my darling, and more pretty clothes than any girl, you could have more beaux, if only—"

"I'd mind my tongue," snapped Andulko. "Well, I'll not! And to show you and everyone I'm not a wallflower, I'll leave this hateful house. I'll go to the square and dance with *someone*—even if he's the Devil himself!"

Before her mother could stop her, Andulko was out of the door and down the flower-bordered path. At the end of the lane she ran toward the square. There old Honza was scraping dance tunes on his fiddle as the lads swung the pretty girls about. Feet flew quicker than eye could follow, petticoats billowed and laughter rang out like bells.

Andulko stood at the edge of the dancers. And though all the boys saw her, none of them paid the slightest attention to her. All knew her waspish ways and had felt the sting of her tongue. Andulko's lip curled in scorn. "You'll notice me when I start dancing," she muttered and entered the inn. Then she seated herself at a table in the corner.

Trappers and hunters stopped at the inn on their way to the mountains. With luck, she'd meet a stranger. Once he'd seen her, he'd invite her to dance, and then— At thought of her triumph, she tapped the toe of her boot, in time to Honza's fiddling.

Andulko was so wrapped up in her own thoughts, she didn't see the handsome young stranger come up behind. She jumped when he whispered, "Will you honor me with the next dance?" And when she glanced up and met his dark glowing eyes, she felt a tinge of uneasiness.

"W-who are you?" faltered Andulko.

"Oh, just a hunter from far away." The young man laughed. "I was passing through the village, and lonely till I saw you," he added, and led Andulko to the square.

The young man, who wore a hunter's green jacket and breeches, whirled Andulko away in his arms. Dance after dance they had together. The village youths gaped and stared. They admitted they'd never seen a handsomer pair. Still—they sniggered. "Poor fellow, he's a stranger. Wait till he gets a taste of Andulko's tongue."

As the hours slipped away, Andulko was so happy she forgot to be nasty. Besides, all at once, she was in love. Her pretty face was flushed with pleasure, her eyes sparkled like diamonds. When old Honza stopped scraping, and put away his fiddle, she sighed. "I wish we could go on dancing forever," she exclaimed, and watched the square empty slowly.

The hunter's dark eyes glowed. "If you really mean that," he said, "we might arrange it, if you'd care to come with me, that is."

"I'd go anywhere with you," Andulko said recklessly. "Tell me, where do you live?"

The hunter laughed softly. But Andulko was too much in love to notice the laugh or the crafty smile that twisted his lips. "If you'll put your arms around my neck, and get on my back," he said. "I'll whisper the name."

Andulko did as she was told. Then a dreadful thing happened. For no sooner had the handsome young hunter whispered the name than he disappeared. In his place stood a dark grinning young Devil with horns and cloven hooves, and a frightening forked tail. And she was clasping his neck! Andulko screamed with fright and tried to let go, but somehow she couldn't. Nor was there anyone about, to hear her cries. "Let me go," she shrieked and kicked wildly.

"Not until we reach the Great Black Gate," chuckled the Devil. "There you'll get all the attention you want!" So saying, he whisked the girl away, with no one in the village the wiser.

Just how they reached the Gate of Hell, Andulko wasn't sure, though she thought they entered a hole in the forest, and then hurtled down, down through a dark passageway. But when the Devil stopped before a gate that loomed black and forbidding, at the heart of the earth, she knew well enough where they were.

"Well, we're here," the Devil shouted. "Now get off my back, foolish girl. Others will look after you now."

"Oh, no, they won't!" shrilled Andulko, so furious she was no longer afraid. She'd teach the cheating two-timing Devil a lesson he'd not forget! If he thought to dump her here like a sack of meal, he'd have another think coming. "I'll not get off until you carry me back to earth—maybe not then," she screamed, with a vicious pinch at the nape of the Devil's neck.

The Devil howled as Andulko continued to screech and pinch, and between them they raised such a commotion that the Black Gate burst open and out leaped a horde of demons, to see what was going on. "Pull the wretched girl off," roared the Devil. "Stoke up the fires."

With wild shrieks the demons fell upon Andulko. They tugged and pulled—first one, then all together. But the harder they tried to get her off the Devil's back, the tighter she clung, the louder she shrieked, the harder she kicked. At last the demons fell back, nursing bruised shins, roaring with pain.

As the tumult rose, the Master Devil himself appeared at the Gate. "What's the meaning of this fracas?" he demanded and waved his pitchfork at Andulko. "Who's she? And you, Devil, what trouble are you in, this time?"

"S-she's only a girl I tricked to the G-Gate," wailed the mortified Devil, doubled over with pain at Andulko's kicks. "How did I know she'd stick like a leech?"

The Master Devil's brow darkened. "So, you've done it again! You've tricked another human here without making a pact first," he thundered. "The last time you muddled I thought I taught

you that even Devils have rules! First the bargaining, the pact, then the tricks!"

The Devil cringed, then broke down completely. "I-I didn't mean it to happen this way," he whined. "But once I'd changed back into a Devil, it was so e-easy to bring the silly girl here. And now I'm well-nigh worn out by the wench," he ended miserably.

"You'll be more worn out, you fool, by the time you've toted her back to earth," bawled the Master, prodding him with his fork. "Get out of my sight. Take her back at once. Get her off your back. And until you do, you're banished from Hell," he added so menacingly the Devil blanched.

Without losing a moment, the young Devil scuttled for the dark passageway. "Ha, ha," jeered Andulko, digging his ribs with her heels. "So you're taking me back to earth, after all, though it may be a long time before you and I part company."

On the way to the hole, the Devil tried to bribe the girl. "Once we're on earth, I'll give you gold, jewels, trunkfuls of dresses—"

"As if they ever did me any good!" sniffed Andulko.

"I'll give you anything," the Devil promised desperately.

Andulko gave him a sharp kick. "If I give you my soul, eh, when I'm ugly and old?" she sneered. "For tricking me, you'll not get off that easily," she went on. "Devil or not, I'll cling to your leathery neck—till I find one more to my liking!"

The girl's mocking laughter gave the Devil an idea and a faint ray of hope. As they reached earth, he was thinking fast. If he could only find some handsome—and unsuspecting—young man!

Before leaving the woods, the Devil changed himself back into human form. Then he stumbled down the long road to the next village. His burden seemed so heavy he was bent over double. He could scarcely drag one foot after the other. He scanned the hills on either side of the road.

But he saw neither farmer nor shepherd nor other human— only the lonely castles, perched like birds of prey on hilltops and rocks, above the valley.

As the Devil rounded a bend in the road, his dull eyes brightened. He straightened up and quickened his step. For there beside the river, a goatherd lolled in the sun, while his Master's beasts scampered over the meadow. The day was warm. The youth had slipped his arms from the sheepskin jacket that now hung from his shoulders, fastened by the top button. "Good day, stranger," called out the disguised Devil. "May I sit beside you and stretch my tired legs? It's weary I am—carrying this woman."

The goatherd glanced up curiously. "Make yourself at home," he said pleasantly. "My name is Jan. It's cool here. But why, since you're so tired, do you carry a woman? She looks healthy and strong."

"Why, indeed?" groaned the Devil, for a warning dig made him wince. He gingerly eased down himself and the girl beside Jan. "This woman refuses to let me go, that's why! I was hunting in the woods yonder, minding my own affairs, when she leaped out at me. Before I could help myself, she'd sprung to my back. 'Carry me to the next village,' she ordered. When I refused, she bit and clawed. I tried to shake her off. I threatened and cajoled. But much good it did me," he ended bitterly. "Here we are and the village is seven miles away!"

Now when Jan, who was a kindhearted youth, heard the trumped-up tale, he was moved to compassion. He began to wonder how he could help the stranger—and still not get himself into a like fix. After a while, his eyes sparkled with merriment. He leaned toward Andulko. "If that stupid fellow could only see how pretty you are," he said, smiling, "he'd carry you without complaint to the end of the world! Now if I had the chance—" he added, groping for the top button on his jacket.

With a little shriek, Andulko sprang to Jan's back. She clutched the empty arms of the sheepskin, then reached eagerly toward his neck. But before she could clasp it, Jan leaped up. He whirled about quickly. With a deft twist at the button and a thrust at the girl, he flung her, screaming, to the middle of the river.

"Quick, quick, before she gets to shore," Jan shouted to the hunter. "We must hide in the bushes beyond the bend."

The girl's screams and threats rent the air as the pair loped toward the bend. "Safe at last!" Jan guffawed, holding his aching sides. "Now the woman will have to carry herself to the village, seven miles away, but I advise you never to let her see you again."

"I'll see to that," his companion said and thanked Jan warmly. "My friend, you don't know the great service you've done me." He continued, "I'm a Devil in disguise, banished from Hell because of her."

"You—a D-Devil!" stammered Jan, falling back in terror.

"You have nothing to fear," the Devil assured him. "On the contrary, I shall reward your kindness. Devil or not, I'm grateful. Now that you've rid me of the woman, I can return to Hell. The Master Devil will forgive me," he concluded, his eyes glowing brightly. "Farewell, my friend, until we meet again."

Jan gaped in astonishment. The next instant the Devil had vanished.

As weeks and then months passed, and the goatherd didn't see the companion of his strange adventure again, Jan began to think he'd dreamed the whole thing. Then one night at dusk while driving home his Master's goats, he suddenly met the Devil face to face.

He stepped out from the shadows, a dark frightening figure, with round bright eyes and a long forked tail that curled over his back. Jan, who'd never seen a Devil before except in human disguise as a hunter, was so terrified, at first, that his teeth chattered, his knees turned to water. "Don't be afraid, dear friend," the Devil said so reassuringly that Jan laughed shakily. "I'm the man you saved from that woman. I've not forgotten your kindness nor what I owe you. And now that the Master's sent me back to earth on a mission, I'm going to see you get your reward."

"But I don't want a reward, not for ducking the girl," protested Jan, feeling quite easy now in the Devil's company.

"Never mind, you'll get it just the same!" The Devil chuckled, immensely pleased with himself. "If you do as I say, you'll be rich—rich enough to buy goats, hire goat boys of your own—and all without the usual fee," he added, winking. He waved a dark hand toward the steep hills that rose on either side. "Do you see those castles on top?" he asked abruptly.

Jan nodded.

"Well then, listen carefully," his companion continued, dropping his voice. "Three nights hence, I'm going to scare the wits out of the Duke who lives in the nearest castle. I'll be there before midnight and you must be there, too." The round eyes burned like lanterns in the gathering gloom, as the Devil went on to explain his scheme. He'd tell the Duke he'd come for his soul, though his time wasn't up for another seven years. Nevertheless, the demon would pretend it was. He'd threaten and abuse the silly fellow till he was confused. "And that's where you come in," he said gleefully. "When the Duke's screaming for mercy, you're to rush to the scene and chase me off, crying, "Devil, Devil, leave at once or things will go badly for you!"

"And then—?" prompted Jan, his eyes sparkling.

"Then I'll vanish," the Devil said. "And the stupid fellow—who'll think *you* saved him—will give you two sacks of gold."

"G-gold! Two sacks of it!" gasped Jan.

"Gold—that's what I said." The Devil snorted delightedly and continued, "But that, my friend, is only half your reward. The second night, at the castle on the adjoining hill, exactly the same thing will happen. When I threaten that Duke and you warn me—and I disappear—you'll get two more bags of gold."

Jan opened his mouth, but the Devil held up his hand. "I must hurry, so listen now," he said. "Heed well what I tell you. The third night, I'll visit the old Duke whose castle is on the crag yonder. His time is up! I'll not be bluffing when I say I've come for his soul. At his castle you mustn't interfere, my friend," he warned so frighteningly that Jan shivered, in spite of himself.

As darkness fell all about, Jan stood alone with his Master's goats.

For Jan, the next three days crawled by like snails. But at last the night of his appointment with the Devil arrived. The goatherd climbed the hill to the castle of the first Duke. Even before he'd peered through the window, Jan heard the demon roar, "Well, are you ready to go?"

"My time's not up and you k-know it," quavered the Duke, so pitifully Jan felt sorry for him. And when the youth pressed his eye close to the windowpane, and saw the Devil lashing his tail and making frightening grimaces, he felt even sorrier.

"Your time's not up, ha?" the Devil bellowed in disgust. "You're too befuddled to count!"

When the Duke screamed for mercy, Jan rushed to the room. "Devil, Devil," he shouted. "Get away, quickly or things will go badly for you!"

The Devil disappeared. And then, as he'd predicted, the grateful Duke—once he'd stopped shaking—took two sacks from his coffers. "These are yours," he said, pressing the gold upon the goatherd. "Your presence of mind saved me from the Devil this night."

Later that evening, lying on his straw mattress in the shed next his Master's kitchen, Jan laughed until tears ran down his cheeks. "Tonight the Duke will sleep soundly as I!" he chuckled and patted the plump sacks at his side.

The following night, at the castle of the second Duke, everything happened exactly as before. When Jan shouted and the Devil disappeared, the second Duke, also, gave the youth two bags of gold. He stowed them away under his cot, along with the others. "Thanks to the Devil, I'm r-rich," he murmured drowsily, stretching out his long legs on the bed. "I'll marry a beautiful girl, buy a farm, raise goats and s-sheep—"

Driving his Master's goats to the hillside, at dawn, Jan was still in a happy daze. "The Devil's a fine fellow," he said. "Tonight I'll tell him so."

Jan was so wrapped up in plans for the future, he was surprised to see a man running toward him. "My Master, the Duke, entreats you to come to the castle on the crag," the messenger gasped. "He's heard of your courage, how you saved two neighboring noblemen from the Devil. The Duke implores your help."

"Tell your Master I cannot help him, alas," said Jan, mindful of the Devil's warning.

When the messenger found he could do nothing to change Jan's mind, he returned to his Master. "I'll go to the goatherd myself," the old Duke said. "Fetch my cloak. Saddle my horse."

After the Duke begged Jan to help him and the youth still refused, he sighed deeply. "I'm wicked and wrinkled," he said. "For my many sins, I deserve punishment in Hell. Yet, now that time's run out, I don't want to go—not without a second chance. I want to stay on earth long enough to right some of the wrongs I've committed. It's too late now unless you'll help me," he concluded sadly. "I'd hoped to succor the widowed, the orphaned, the weak—those I've defrauded these many years. I want to return the lands, the cattle, the tithes I've exacted from tenant farmers."

Jan stroked his chin. The Duke's repentance was genuine. Yet, after what the Devil had said, if he, Jan, interfered, he could expect no mercy. "If you mean what you say," he said at last, "I'll help you. But I'll go to Hell, instead of you, if I fail."

"And if you succeed," cried the Duke, "you shall be my son! You'll marry my daughter, the beautiful Ludmilla, inherit my dukedom, my fortune, and restore peace to the heart of a wicked old man," he added gratefully.

"Until tonight, farewell. I must think now," said Jan.

When Jan arrived at the castle, shortly before midnight, the moon was shining brightly. He was astonished to see the courtyard filled with people—sullen farmers and their wives and children—all clamoring to see the Devil carry away the Duke. "Tonight the wicked old man will get his deserts," they muttered, one to another.

As the chimes in the valley began to strike twelve, Jan heard the Devil rasp, "Follow me through the door, old man. Don't make a fuss. You've had your fun. Your people are in the courtyard waiting to tear you apart. But don't be afraid," he added with a sneer. "I'll drag you off before they hurt you!"

Jan rushed to the room. There stood the Duke before the hearth, his face pale, his manner calm. "I shall make no fuss, Devil—nor am I afraid," he was saying. "I'll follow. You lead."

"Devil, Devil," yelled Jan. "Quick, quick, you must leave! Otherwise things will go hard with you."

"Idiot! Knucklehead! How dare you?" the Devil roared. "I warned you not to interfere tonight. I told you the consequences." Glaring at Jan, he shot out an arm.

Jan stepped aside nimbly. "Listen, you fool!" he bellowed. "I'm here to warn you of danger—not to save that worthless Duke. Outside, in the crowd, I saw the woman! She's waiting for you, waiting to leap on your back the instant you walk through the door. Once she gets her arms around your neck, she'll not let go again!"

The Devil didn't wait to hear more. With a wild howl, he was up the chimney and far away, before the Duke could turn to thank Jan. "You have given me a second chance, my son," he said and embraced the goatherd, tears of gratitude in his eyes.

Now when the people learned how the brave youth had rescued the Duke so he could make amends to them, they tossed up their caps and shouted themselves hoarse. "Long live the Duke! Long live the goatherd, Jan!" they cried. And when the Duke led out the lovely Ludmilla and placed her small hand between the youth's firm palms, their joy was boundless. "The young Duke will look after us—once the old Duke dies," declared the people.

But the old Duke didn't die—at least, not until he reached the age of a hundred and seven. And when he did, angels carried his soul to Paradise.

To follow the old Duke wasn't easy, for he'd made good his promises to those he'd oppressed. But when Jan and Ludmilla took over the dukedom, they governed so justly and well that everyone loved them.

And as for Andulko, no one is certain what happened to her. Some claim that a girl answering her description turned up, wet and bedraggled, in a certain village, seven miles from a deep river. She settled in the village, in a deserted hut. There are those who think she became a horrid witch. Others say a widowed farmer took pity on the girl and married her. "But he lived to rue the day," they add. "He soon discovered that his wife had a nasty tongue— and an even nastier temper!"

The Author

DOROTHY GLADYS SPICER is a New Yorker, "since the early seventeenth century," she says, "when a Dutch sailmaker from Hoorn emigrated to New Amsterdam."

Miss Spicer was graduated from Vassar, and from Radcliffe, where she majored in art history and archaeology. She is a folklorist, well-known for her stories and work in peasant crafts and folk backgrounds. She has studied arts *and* native festivals in towns and villages of Europe and the Orient, where she has carried on special research under folklore experts of the various countries.

She now lives in White Plains, New York, and is author of many books and articles on folk festivals, customs, and foods. Included among her eighteen books are, *46 Days of Christmas, 13 Witches, 13 Monsters, 13 Ghosts, and 13 Giants.*